ANGELS & DEMONS

ANGELS & DEMONS

LAURA (L.A.) MARIANI

The PEOPLE ALCHEMIST

BOOKS BY LAURA (L.A.)MARIANI

Angels & Demons

The Fallen Angel

The Hot Ghost

The Bad Saint

The Fallen Hero

The Hot Priest

The Bad Santa

Untamed Hearts

The BAD Boy

The BAD Girl

Holiday Romance

14 Days to Love Series: Short Sweet Steamy

Parisian Serendipity

Venetian Whispers

Mumbay Surprise

Romeo in Rome

New York Melody

Artic Embrace

Santorini Sunsets

Havana Heat

Barcelona Dreams

Marrakesh Magic

Vienna Waltz

Sydney Sparks

Amsterdam Affair

Cape Town Safari

Box Set

14 Days to Love: Short Sweet Steamy

Twelve Days of Christmas Series

A Partridge in a Pear Tree: Hot Spicy Christmas Novella

Two Turtle Doves: Hot Spicy Christmas Novella

Three French Hens: Hot Spicy Christmas Novella

Four Calling Birds: Hot Spicy Christmas Novella

Five Golden Rings: Hot Spicy Christmas Novella

Six Geese a-Laying: Hot Spicy Christmas Novella

Seven Swans a-Swimming: Hot Spicy Christmas Novella

Eight Maids a-Milking: Hot Spicy Christmas Novella

Nine Ladies Dancing: Hot Spicy Christmas Novella

Ten Lords a-Leaping: Hot Spicy Christmas Novella

Eleven Pipers Piping: Hot Spicy Christmas Novella

Twelve Drummers Drumming: Hot Spicy Christmas Novella

Box Set

Twelve Days of Christmas

Shadowbrook Paranormal Series

A Halloween Romance: Enchanted in Shadowbrook

The Midnight Hour:A Halloween Shadowbrook Romance

Navy Seals Hunks Series

SEALed Hearts

SEALed with a Kiss

SEALed Undercover

SEALed Pursuit

SEALed Love Code

SEALed beyond Duty

Box Set

Navy SEAL Hunks

A Royal Romance Trilogy

A Coronation Weekend Romance

The Wicked Princess

The Lost Kingdom

Box Set

A Royal Romance Trilogy

The Nine Lives of Gabrielle Series

Gabrielle (prequel/first in series)

Her Little Secret (series spin off)

For Three She Plays

A New York Adventure

Searching for Goren

Tasting Freedom

For Three She Strays

Paris Toujours Paris

Me Myself and Us

Freedom Over Me

For Three She Stays

London Calling

Back in Your Arms

The Greatest Love

ISBN: 978-1-917104-33-3

CONTENTS

FOREWORD

Angels & Demons is a collection of OTT insta-love steamy romance novellas that are intended for a mature audience. If you crave a fast-paced, passionate read, jump right in!

Angels & Demons Series

The Fallen Angel
The Hot Ghost
The Bad Saint
The Fallen Hero
The Hot Priest
The Bad Santa

THE FALLEN ANGEL

PROLOGUE

LUCIAN

Plink. Plip. Plop.

Rain splish splashes on the old cobblestones. It's October again. The month when the veil between worlds narrows, when I'm granted the bittersweet taste of the mortal realm. I glide through the autumn mist, my feet barely touching the ground. The mortals rush past me, oblivious to my presence. Their unseeing eyes slide right over me as if I'm nothing but a wisp of fog.

A young woman catches my eye. Golden hair glowing like a halo in the twilight, luscious curves wrapped in a thin rain-coat, full ruby lips.

"Stop it, Lucian!" I sigh, running a hand through my raven-dark hair, my red wings flip-flapping in the wind. For a moment, I allow myself to imagine she can perceive me. "This is exactly what brought you down, a shadow among shadows." Memories wash over me, tides of shame and regret, back to that fateful day when I was consumed by unholy craving. I close my eyes, remembering her porcelain skin, her sweet blue eyes wide with innocence. The way she trembled beneath my touch as I led her into temptation and possessed her. Her big luscious t... "Stop, stop, stop it!" my fists clenched down my sides. "Arrogant, lustful fool."

A child skips by and, just for an instant, stops as if looking at me. My breath catches.

"Damien," his mother says, pulling. "Let's go. We are late." The moment is lost. I continue to roam the cobbled streets, aimlessly, weaving in between the blissfully unaware mortals. All around me doorsteps and windows are full of Halloween decorations. The scent of cinnamon and salted caramel fills the air.

Another October, another fleeting chance at redemption. But I fear my soul is far too tarnished. Only a pure heart can perceive me now. Only an act of true selflessness can wash away my sins.

Perhaps one day I'll find it. That elusive, pure heart who can free me. But for now, I am caught between worlds, paying the price for my transgression.

I am Lucian, the fallen one.

CAN YOU SEE ME?

LUCIAN

L ondon's streets stretch before me, a labyrinth I've crossed countless times. I pause for a minute under a flickering streetlamp catching my reflection in a nearby shop window —alabaster skin, eyes as dark as the void, and hair the color of midnight.

The rush of mortals swirls around me. Their laughter, sorrows, petty concerns wash over me like waves on sand. I stopped long ago trying to understand these fleeting creatures whose lives burn bright and fast.

I continue wandering, aimlessly, lost in memories, my sin heavy upon my shoulders. Today I can feel the weight of my fall from grace pressing upon me with renewed intensity. I remember the face of the virgin I seduced, the catalyst for my downfall. Her wide, innocent eyes still haunt me.

"Aaaaah!"

. . .

I walk around the corner into a dimly lit alley, my footsteps silent on the cobblestones. There I see a young woman, on the floor, cornered by two leering men.

"Please," she begs, her voice trembling. "I don't want any trouble," her big green eyes wide like a deer caught in a head-light. She is so beautiful and sinfully luscious.

"Damn it, Lucian," I remind myself, "not a good time for this."

"Should've thought of that before wandering down here, love," one of the men laughs, a harsh, grating sound.

I position myself between the woman and her assailants. The men look right through me, gazes fixed on their intended victim.

"Who... who are you?" the woman's voice stops me cold, her eyes locked on me. Those big emerald eyes ...

Can she ... ? Impossible. Unless...

"You can ... see me?" I ask, momentarily forgetting the danger at hand.

. . .

"Of course I can, " she answers confused. "Why wouldn't I?"

"Who are you talking to bitch?" One of the men growls.

"She is cuckoo," the other replies, "don't matter. Get her!"

They start moving forward, closing in on her. I act on instinct. The air crackles, and the alley is bathed in an eerie, ethereal light and turbine wind, thrusting them backward, terror etched on their faces. "What the fuck?" one of them cries out.

I step forward, my wings unfurling behind me. "Leave," I bark, but my voice resounds like thunder.

They run, tripping over themselves in their haste to escape. I turn back to the woman as they disappear around the corner, reining in my power. She is on the floor, wide-eyed but unafraid, her eyes filled with wonder rather than terror.

"Are you alright?" I ask softly not to scare her.

She nods as she pulls herself up, a tiny smile playing at the corners of her lips. "I am," she whispers. "Thanks to you. It's Eva. And you are...?" She extends her hand.

Do we shake hands? Better not.

· · ·

"Lucian," I reply, the name feeling strange on my tongue in this context. "How can you see me, Eva?" I blurt out confused.

"What do you mean?" she answers, perplexed, furrowing her brow and tilting her head. "You're standing right in front of me."

Only the very pure of heart can see me in my non-corporeal form. But how could such a pure soul exist in this sinful city? I study her, trying to understand ....Her gorgeous curves are made for sin... They are made for me.

"You should go home," I say, trying to compose myself. "It's not safe out here."

"You saved me," she says softly, coming dangerously close to me. I am transfixed by the depth of her eyes. And the sweet smell of jasmine wafting from her hair ... and those pink, plump lips ... and ...

Lucian, get a grip. I should disappear, vanish back into the shadows where I belong. Desire stirs within me, a hungry, insistent thing that I struggle to suppress. I want her.

"Stop it, Lucian ... not again," I mumble.

"I beg your pardon?" she looks confused.

· · ·

"I... I should go," I stammer. I forgot she could hear me.

Eva reaches out, her fingers slightly touching my arm. I'm hard already.

Sweet. Intoxicating. I know I should walk away. I must. This woman is the very thing that could damn me for eternity.

But as I look into her eyes, I concede, can't help myself, "Let me walk you home." She smiles. I can see her pink tongue between her slightly parted lips. I just want to ravish that tongue, taste her...

I fear the emotions this woman stirs within me, fear succumbing again to the very sins that led to my downfall.

As we walk, Eva's voice yanks me from my tumultuous thoughts. "So, Lucian," she asks playfully, "do you often swoop in to rescue damsels in distress?"

"No, not typically." I can't help but chuckle. "You caught me on an unusually heroic night."

She giggles; God, I am so turned on. "I'm glad you made an exception..." she continues and then shudders as if thinking about what could have happened.

. . .

"You shouldn't be out alone at night," I scold her gently. "It's dangerous."

"I can take care of myself!" She says defiant. If looks could kill.

I look at her sternly, "Well, tonight was just... an off night," she adds quickly.

Her spirit impresses me, even as it worries me. "I'm sure. Even so, caution is wise. The world can be a dark place."

"You sound like you're speaking from experience," her eyes never leaving mine.

"You could say that," I reply cryptically.

"So, how did you do that back there?" She leans forward slightly. "You know, with the thunder, light and the... wings thingy?"

"You saw that?" I reply, caught off guard by her directness.

"It was incredible," she nods. "For a moment, you looked... well, not human."

. . .

I debate how to respond. The truth is out of the question, but I don't want to lie to her. "It's... complicated," I say instead, buying time.

Eva raises an eyebrow. "What's so complicated about it?"

I turn to her, bracing myself. "What would you say," I begin cautiously, "if I told you I wasn't human?"

She scans me for a long moment, her expression unreadable. Then, to my surprise, she smiles. "I'd say that explains a lot. Are you an angel?"

"What makes you think that?"

"Beside the wings?" Eva shrugs, chuckling. "You have this... I don't know; it's hard to explain," she says, curious and intrigued.

"Angel? No, not quite." I hesitate. "But I was once... close to them."

Her eyes widen, but her expression doesn't betray any fear. "A fallen angel?" she exclaims.

"I am," and I nod, resigned.

TEMPTATION

LUCIAN

I can't tear my eyes away from her as we walk side by side. She is a vision of mortal perfection that threatens to undo centuries of carefully constructed walls. Her luscious curves beckon like the sweetest temptation, accentuated by the simple coat clinging to her form. Waves of red hair cascade over her shoulders, framing a face that could make the heavens weep with envy. But it's her eyes that grip me - wide, innocent pools of deepest green that shine with an inner light I haven't seen since...since before my fall.

My hands clench at my sides as I wrestle with the urge to reach out and touch her porcelain skin, to claim those full lips with my own. Every instinct screams at me to make her mine, to mark her as my territory, and never let her go. The alpha in me roars to dominate, to possess.

But I can't. I won't.

. . .

"You're...you're really an angel," Eva whispers, her voice filled with awe rather than fear.

I shift uncomfortably, unused to being so exposed. "Fallen angel," I correct her gruffly. "There's a difference."

She takes a step closer, and I have to steel myself not to retreat. Or worse, to grab her and never let go.

"But you saved me," she says softly. "The attackers...you stopped them. How can you be fallen if you still do good?"

I bark out a harsh laugh. "Trust me, sweetheart, I'm no saint. One good deed doesn't erase my sin."

Her brow furrows adorably, and I'm struck by an overwhelming urge to smooth it with my thumb, to caress her cheek and draw her close. I clench my fists tighter, nails biting into my palms.

"I don't believe that," Eva says with quiet conviction. "There's good in you, Lucian. I can feel it."

Oh, if she only knew the decidedly ungood thoughts racing through my mind right now. I imagine pressing her against the wall, my body flushing against hers and devouring those tempting lips. In my fantasy, she melts against me, soft and pliant as I explore every lush curve. I picture lifting her, her legs wrapping around my waist as I carry her to bed and...

No. Stop. I can't let myself go down that road. I won't make that mistake again, no matter how much every fiber of my being aches to claim her. I can't.

"You don't know what you're talking about," I growl, turning away from her. "I'm beyond redemption."

"I don't believe that," Eva repeats, more firmly this time. She reaches out, her small hand resting on my arm. The touch sears through me like a holy fire, and it takes every ounce of willpower not to spin around and crush her to me.

Instead, I jerk away, putting distance between us. "You should be afraid of me," I snarl. "I'm not some fluffy guardian angel."

"I'm not afraid," she smiles. "I trust you."

Her words hit me like a physical blow. Trust is a fragile, precious thing that I haven't experienced before. And here she is using it so freely, so innocently. It makes me want to wrap her in my arms and shield her from all the darkness in the world—including my own.

"You shouldn't," I mutter, running a hand through my hair in frustration. "Trusting me will only lead to pain."

. . .

Eva takes another step closer, and I have to fight the urge to back away. Or to close the distance between us entirely.

"Maybe," she says softly. "But I choose to believe in second chances. In redemption. Even for the fallen."

For a moment, I allow myself to imagine what it would be like to be worthy of the trust shining in Eva's eyes and to feel the warmth of the flesh once more.

But I know the price of giving in to a fleeting moment of mortal passion. Damnation.

And yet...looking at Eva, bathed in the soft glow of twilight, I find myself wondering if it might be worth it.

"You're playing with fire, little one," I warn her, my voice rough with suppressed desire.

She meets my eyes unflinchingly. The air between us crackles. I can hear her heart racing and smell the subtle shift in her scent that speaks of arousal. It would be so easy to give in, to take what she's all but offering. My body screams for it, every muscle coiled tight with the need to possess her.

. . .

I take a step back, then another. "Forget about me Eva," I say, my voice cold.

Hurt flashes in her eyes. "I can't do that," she responds. "And I don't think you want me to, either."

She's right, damn her. The thought of never seeing her again, of those eyes looking at another man ... it makes me want to howl with rage and grief. What am I doing? I am not even a man anymore ...

"What I want doesn't matter," I say flatly.

Eva opens her mouth to argue, but I'm done. With a thought, I unfurl my wings, great, shadowy things that fill the alley. Her eyes widen in awe, and I let myself bask in her admiration for a moment. Then I launch myself skyward, leaving her far behind.

As I soar above the city, I try to convince myself I've done the right thing. Pushing her away is the only way to keep her safe —from me, from the consequences of loving a fallen angel.

But even as I rise higher, I can feel the tether of her presence pulling me back. And I know, with a certainty that terrifies me, that this isn't over.

. . .

One way or another, Eva will be my salvation...or my final damnation.

I MET SOMEONE
EVA

A faint ray of sunshine breaks through my curtains, "It was just a dream," I whisper to my empty bedroom. "It couldn't have been real." But the lingering ache in my muscles tells me something definitely real happened, my heart racing as if I've just run a marathon. The events of last night flood back, vivid and surreal.

I close my eyes, savoring the image—tall and muscular, with a chiseled jaw that could cut glass. But it was his eyes that haunted me—deep, dark pools that seemed to hold centuries of secrets. Lucian was not like I'd ever imagined angels would be.

"Stop it, Eva," I rebuke, opening my eyes. "He's gone. You'll never see him again."

The thought sends a twinge through my chest. I try to shake it off as I stumble out of bed and into the shower. The hot water does little to clear my head. If anything, it makes Lucian's presence feel more visceral. I can almost feel his strong arms shielding me from harm. Or were they wings? Did he...?

"Get a grip," I mutter, shutting off the water. "He's an angel, a fallen angel for crying out loud. Not exactly boyfriend material."

Still, I can't help but wonder what it would be like to run my fingers through his tousled dark hair. To trace the lines of his face, feel the rough stubble on his jaw.

"You're pathetic, Eva," I thump my head against the mirror. "Absolutely pathetic."

My phone buzzes, snapping me out of my Lucian-induced haze.

"Still on for coffee?"

Oops, I'd forgotten entirely about Mia.

"You never called me back last night!"

"So sorry! Yes, it's definitely still on. See you later."

I potter through the rest of my day. When I step outside my apartment building, a familiar chill runs down my spine. The same feeling I had last night, right before those men attacked me.

I look around, scanning the street. Nothing unusual, but I can't shake the sensation of being watched.

"You're just paranoid," I mumble, "Keep walking, Eva." But the feeling persists. I make my way to the coffee shop; every shadow seems menacing, every passerby is a potential threat. I find myself longing for Lucian's presence, for the safety of his arms.

The bell above the door chimes as I enter the café. Mia waves from our usual corner table, two steaming mugs already waiting.

"There you are!" she exclaims as I slide into the comfy chair. "I was starting to worry. What's wrong?"

"Wrong?" I reply, trying to act surprised.

"I don't know," Mia tilts her head. "You look ... flustered? Did something happen last night?" She is studying me, her Mrs Marple's skills in full flow. Flustered. Well, You would be, too, if you'd met an angel.

. . .

For a moment, I consider telling her everything. The attack, Lucian and angels being real. But the words die in my throat. How could I possibly?

"Nothing major," I lie. "Just had trouble sleeping."

Mia's eyes narrow. She knows me too well to buy that excuse. "Eva..."

I sigh, wrapping my hands around the warm mug. "Okay, fine. I... met someone."

It's not entirely a lie. Mia's eyes light up. "Ooh, details! Who is he? Where did you meet? Is he cute?"

I can't help but laugh at her enthusiasm. "His name is Lucian. We met... unexpectedly. And yes, he's..." I trail off, searching for words to describe Lucian's otherworldly handsomeness.

"That hot, huh?" Mia grins. "When are you seeing him again?"

The smile fades from my face. "I'm not. It was just a one-time thing."

Mia's face falls. "Oh, Eva. I'm sorry. Was he a jerk?"

· · ·

I shake my head quickly. "No, no. He was... incredible. It's complicated."

"Complicated how?" Mia presses. "If he's so great, why not see him again?"

I stare into my coffee, wishing I could tell her the truth. That Lucian isn't just some guy. Being with him would probably be the worst idea in the history of bad ideas. Not that he wants to. He made THAT perfectly clear.

"He's just... not available," I say finally. It's the closest thing to the truth I can manage.

Mia reaches across the table, squeezing my hand. "I'm sorry, sweetie. His loss."

I manage a weak smile. "Thanks. Can we talk about something else?"

Mia launches into a story about her latest Tinder disaster, but I find myself only half-listening. My mind keeps drifting back to Lucian, to the way his touch sent electricity coursing through my veins, to the raw power I sensed beneath his calm exterior. I never felt like that before. I would have even DONE it! Imagine that, my first time. With an angel!

. . .

"Earth to Eva!" Mia's voice cuts through my daydream. "Where'd you go?"

I blink, forcing myself back to the present. "Sorry, I guess I'm more tired than I thought."

Mia's brow furrows with concern. "Maybe you should go home and rest. We can do this another time."

Part of me wants to protest, to cling to the normalcy. But the weight of last night's events is pressing down on me, making it hard to focus.

"You're probably right," I admit. "Rain check?"

Mia nods, giving me another worried look as I gather my things. "Call me if you need anything, okay?"

I promise I will, though we both know it's unlikely. I've always been the type to deal with my problems alone, even when I'm in way over my head.

That prickle of unease returns full force as I return onto the bustling sidewalk. I scan the crowd, half-expecting to see Lucian's striking figure. But there's no sign of him.

· · ·

"Get it together," I mutter, forcing myself to keep walking. "He's not coming back."

But even as I say the words, I can't quite bring myself to believe them. Something in the way Lucian looked at me went beyond mere protection. A hunger, a longing that matched my own.

I shake my head, trying to clear it. This is insane. I met the 'guy' once under extreme circumstances. I don't know anything about him other than the fact that he's a freaking fallen angel. I should be terrified, not... whatever this is.

As I round the corner onto my street, some movement catches my eye. I whirl around, my heart pounding. But there's nothing there. Just an empty alley, shadows dancing in the early evening light.

"You're losing it," I whisper, but I can't shake the feeling that I'm being watched. Followed.

I pick up my pace, fumbling for my keys as I approach my building. A hand clamps down on my shoulder as I reach the front steps.

I scream, spinning around with my keys clutched between my knuckles, ready to strike. But the face I see stops me cold.

FOREVER FALLEN
LUCIAN

A scream pierces the dark, slicing through my silent vigil. I snap to attention, my wings unfurling instinctively as I zero in on the source. There, in the shadows of a secluded car park, two men are dragging a struggling woman from their vehicle. Even from this distance, I recognize her instantly. Eva.

My fists clench as I watch them paw at her clothes, their leering faces illuminated by the dim glow of a nearby streetlamp. Eva's terror is palpable, her desperate cries echoing off the concrete walls. She knows no one can hear her. No one human, at least.

Something snaps inside me. In an instant, I'm there, materializing between Eva and her attackers in a blaze of light. My wings spread to their full span, casting massive shadows across the lot. The men stumble back, mouths agape in shock and growing terror.

· · ·

"What the f-" one of them starts to say, but I cut him off with a thunderous voice that reverberates through their very souls.

"HOW DARE YOU LAY YOUR FILTHY HANDS ON HER?" My eyes are blazing like twin suns.

They fall to their knees, cowering and whimpering pathetically. I can smell the acrid stench of their fear, their bodies trembling uncontrollably. Good. Let them be afraid.

"P-please," one of them stammers, "We didn't... we didn't know..."

I take a menacing step forward, and they scramble backward on all fours like terrified animals.

"If I ever see either of you again," I say, my voice dropping to a deadly whisper, "if I even catch a whisper of you near her again or harming another soul, I will drag you screaming into the depths of Hell. Do you understand?"

They nod frantically, tears streaming down their faces.

"Now go," I command, "And pray I forget your faces."

They don't need to be told twice. They scramble to their feet and run, nearly tripping over themselves in their haste to escape.

What have I done? I revealed myself to mortals. I am damned forever now. But when I turn and look at Eva nothing else matters. She's huddled on the ground, her clothes torn and disheveled, her body wracked with sobs.

"Eva," I say softly, kneeling beside her. "It's alright now. You're safe."

She looks up at me, her eyes wide. I hesitate, slowly extending my wings, enveloping her in their soft, protective embrace. "I've got you," I murmur, tightening my hold on her. "You're safe now. Let's get you home."

She nods, still dazed, and I carefully lift her into my arms. With a powerful beat of my wings, we're airborne, soaring above the twinkling lights of London.

Eva clings to me tightly, her face buried against my chest. I can feel her heart racing and smell the lingering fear and adrenaline on her skin. But there's something else, too—a scent that's uniquely hers, intoxicating and pure.

We land on the balcony of her flat, and I gently set her down. Eva stumbles slightly, and I steady her with a hand on her arm. The contact sends a jolt through me, and I quickly pull away.

. . .

"I don't know what would have happened if you hadn't..." Eva whispers, her voice trembling. She trails off, fresh tears welling in her eyes. Before I can stop myself, I'm pulling her into my arms, my wings wrapping around us like a cocoon. God forgive me, I want her.

"Shh," I soothe, stroking her hair. "It's over now. They can't hurt you anymore."

Eva clings to me, her body shaking with silent sobs. I hold her close, marveling at how small and fragile she feels in my arms. How long has it been since I've allowed myself to feel... anything? Did I ever … beside lust?

As her sobs subside, Eva pulls back slightly, looking up at me with those impossibly green eyes. "Why were you there? Have you been watching me?"

I swallow hard, guilt warring with the undeniable pull I feel towards her. "I wanted to protect you. Sorry I was late."

"Protect me?"

"I... yes. You're special."

Eva's brow furrows. "I'm not special. I'm just... me."

. . .

Oh, if she could see herself through my eyes – she's the most extraordinary creature I've ever seen in all my centuries.

But I can't tell her that. Not yet. Maybe not ever.

"You should get some rest," I say, gently guiding her toward the sliding glass door. "It's been a traumatic night."

Eva nods, but as I turn to go, she grabs my hand. "Wait! Will I... will I see you again?"

The longing in her voice matches the ache in my own heart. I know I should maintain my distance. But looking into those pleading eyes, I find myself powerless to resist.

"I'll be here," I promise. "Whenever you need me."

Relief washes over her face, and before I can react, she's throwing herself into my arms. Her lips find mine in a desperate kiss that sets every nerve in my body on fire.

For a moment, I lose myself in the sensation. The softness of her lips, the warmth of her body pressed against mine. But then reality comes crashing back, and I gently push her away.

. . .

"Eva, we can't," I say, my voice rough with desire and regret. "I can't."

Hurt flashes across her face, quickly replaced by embarrassment. "I'm sorry, I shouldn't have... I don't know what came over me."

"It's alright," I assure her, even as every fiber of my being screams to pull her close again. "You've been through a lot tonight. You should get some sleep."

Eva nods, wrapping her arms around herself. "Will you... will you stay? Just until I fall asleep?"

I know I should refuse. But the thought of leaving her alone after everything that's happened is unbearable. "Of course," I hear myself say.

We settle onto her bed, Eva curling up against my side as I wrap a protective wing around her. Within minutes, her breathing evens out as exhaustion finally overtakes her.

I lie there, listening to the steady rhythm of her heartbeat and breathing in her intoxicating scent. My body hums with unfamiliar sensations—desire, protectiveness, and something dangerously close to love. Too close.

· · ·

I allow myself to admit the truth I've been fighting since I first laid eyes on her.

Eva is the love of my life. My soulmate. The other half of my very being.

If only I had met her lifetimes ago when I was still human. But it's too late for that now. All I can do is protect her from afar, never letting her know the depths of my feelings.

It will be the hardest thing I've ever done. But for Eva, I would endure any torment.

She sleeps peacefully now, her hair fanned across her pillow. My chest aches with longing, love, and lingering rage at those who tried to harm her. I'd wanted to destroy them, to rain down my wrath. But I'd held back, for her.

"I will protect you always," I whisper.

I drift as if in a sea of white feathers, "Lucian, it is time to come home, "a familiar voice cuts through the blissful haze. The world tilts and blurs. I'm being pulled away, Eva fading like mist.

"No!" I cry out, clawing desperately to stay. "I won't leave her!"

· · ·

"As you wish..."

I jolt awake with a scream, disoriented. My wings... they're gone, my now all-too-human heart pounding. Moonlight spills through the window as I struggle to calm my ragged breathing.

I'm still here. Still fallen, but here.

EPILOGUE

E va looks like a vision, clad in a gown of shimmering silk that hugs her gorgeous curves to perfection. She is my Heaven on Earth. My bride.

"God, you look so beautiful!" I ache with a profound longing that consumes me whole. Tonight, I will claim her as my own —finally. Forever.

She smiles softly. Innocent, pure, untouched by anyone.

I am burning with desire; I have yearned for this moment since I first saw her. To possess her completely and to taste the sweetness of her skin. To hear her moans of pleasure as I plunge into her over and over and over. I brush away a stray lock of hair from her face, tracing the line of her jaw.

Eva quivers under my touch, her cheeks a deep shade of red.

. . .

"I am yours, Lucian," she gasps. Her voice is trembling as I begin to undress her. I revel in each and every delicious inch of her porcelain skin. I slowly lick and nibble down her neck. "Everything is yours," her arousal growing. I worship her breasts teasingly, circling her hardened nipples with my tongue before suckling them hard into the depths of my mouth.

My hands roam, tracing the contours of her body with a growing hunger. I graze her hip bones, the dip of her waist, and then let my fingers venture lower still, teasing and torturing the damp folds between her thighs. One finger. Two fingers.

"Lucian," Eva arches her back, whimpering in need as I continue to tease her intimate flesh. She is so wet.

"Please," she begs. "I need you, Lucian. Now." Her voice is cracking with desire.

Hearing my name on her lips drives me wild. I pull away from her to free my hard and throbbing cock, jutting outward from my loins.

"Tonight, my love," I rasp, my voice a low growl, "I will make you mine forever and ever. Till our deaths do us part."

. . .

Eva grips my arms more tightly and nods her assent. I push her thighs apart, positioning myself at her entrance.

"I am yours, Eva," I whisper hoarsely.

And with a single, searing thrust, I finally claim her as my own. Falling forever in her depth.

THE HOT GHOST

PROLOGUE

ETHAN

The candelabra flick-flickers and eerie shadows cast across faded tapestries. "Good morning, Ethan," I mutter, drifting through the foyer. "How long has it been since I've heard another soul speak?" My voice echoes through the empty manor, my ethereal form barely disturbs the dust. "Months? Years?" My haunting has been far too successful. Another dreary day begins. I'm bored.

I float up the sweeping staircase. At the top, I pause before a cracked mirror, studying my spectral reflection. "God, I am hot, even if I say so myself." Translucent yet still handsome, frozen forever as the dashing lord I once was. What I wouldn't give to feel again, taste wine on my lips, a good fuck. I miss a good fuck.

I look at the overgrown grounds of the estate. The boundaries shimmer faintly—an invisible barrier I can never cross— beyond a world that has long since moved on without me. The sun is low on the horizon, the sky orange and pink.

. . .

I turn away from the window, gliding through the dusty halls. The portraits of my ancestors watch me with unseeing eyes as I pass. I've memorized every brush stroke, every faded color. "Another riveting conversation, Lord Black-wood?" I quip to a particularly stern-looking portrait. "You're as charming as ever."

I make my way to the grand ballroom, once the jewel of the estate. I close my eyes, and for a moment, I can almost hear the music, the laughter and the swish of silk gowns against the polished floor.

"Enough of this foolishness," I say coming to an abrupt halt.

A creaking floorboard snaps me from my brooding. A voice drifts up from below - an intruder! My lips curl into a sinister grin. At last, some entertainment today.

"Time to give my guest a proper welcome!"

MR GHOST

CHLOE

C *reak, creak.*

I push the creak-creaking front door open. "Well, hello there, spooky mansion!" I can't help but grin. "I am Chloe, and we're going to be great friends," I announce to the empty house. My voice echoes off the high ceilings. This old colonial house is everything I've ever dreamed of. And, if the rumors are true, there's a resident ghost too. I can't believe it; I bagged a haunted house. And just in time for Halloween. I drop the last box with a gratifying thud and turn around, taking in the grand foyer with its peeling wallpaper and dusty chandelier.

I feel a chill down my spine and I swear I can hear a faint whisper in response. My grin widens. "Oh, is that you, Mr. Ghost? Don't be shy now. I'm your new roomie!"

. . .

I start by opening the windows for fresh air and get on with some cleaning before unpacking, humming a jaunty tune as I work. As I arrange my collection of vintage horror movie posters, I catch a glimpse of movement in the dusty mirror hanging on the wall. I whirl around, but the room is empty.

"Playing hide and seek, are we?" I chuckle, turning back to the mirror. "You'll have to try harder than that! Much harder."

The image in the mirror starts to shift and I find myself staring at the reflection of a man. And not just any man – a drop-dead gorgeous specter with chiseled features, tousled dark hair, and piercing blue eyes. Oh, and he's shirtless because, of course, he is. Good Lord, can you be turned on by a ghost?

"Well, hello there, handsome," I say quirking an eyebrow at the apparition. The ghost's eyes widen in surprise clearly not used to this reaction. He opens his mouth as if to speak, but no sound comes out.

"Cat got your tongue?" I tease, turning to face the empty room again. "Or should I say, ectoplasm got your vocal cords?"

A book flies off the shelf, narrowly missing my head. I duck, laughing. "Ooh, temper, temper! You know, there are better ways to get a girl's attention." I walk over to the fallen book and pick it up, dusting off the cover. "'The Complete Works of Edgar Allan Poe.' Nice choice, very on-brand for a haunted house."

. . .

The temperature in the room suddenly drops, and I can see my breath misting in the air. "Brr! Is this your way of asking me to put on a sweater? Because I gotta say, you're the one half-naked here, not me."

I swear I hear a frustrated growl, and the chandelier above me starts to sway ominously. I look up at it, hands on my hips. "Really? The old 'menacing light fixture' trick? Come on, you can do better than that."

Suddenly, all the candles in the room ignite at once, casting eerie shadows on the walls. I clap my hands in delight. "Now that's more like it! Very atmospheric. You're really nailing this whole haunted house vibe."

I flop down on the dusty old sofa, sending up a cloud of particles that dance in the candlelight. "So, do you have a name, or should I just keep calling you 'ghostie'?"

The mirror fogs up, and letters appear as if traced by an invisible finger. E-T-H-A-N.

"Ethan? That's a nice name. I'm Chloe, but you probably already knew that from all my yammering." I wave at the mirror. "Nice to officially meet you, Ethan. I hope you don't mind me moving in on your territory."

. . .

The mirror fogs up again. GET OUT.

I laugh, shaking my head. "Sorry, buddy, no can do. I've signed a lease and everything. Looks like you're stuck with me."

Wind stars blow through the room, ruffling my hair and sending papers flying around. I just sit there, grinning. "If you wanted to play hairdresser, you could've just asked," I say unperturbed. "I like my parting on the left if you don't mind."

I stand up and start gathering the scattered papers. "Look, Ethan, I get it. You're used to being the big, bad ghost of the house. But here's the thing – I'm not scared. In fact, I think this is all pretty cool."

The candles flicker, and I can feel his presence right behind me. I turn slowly, and there he is – Ethan, in all his translucent glory, standing just inches away from me. Up close, he's even more stunning, with a strong jaw, full lips, and those intense blue eyes that see right through me. I hope he can't read minds…

"Hello again," I say, my voice a little breathier than I'd like to admit. "Decided to show yourself properly, huh?" Now, I am definitely turned on.

Ethan's brow furrows menacingly and he opens his mouth

again. This time, an echoing voice emerges. "Why aren't you afraid?"

I shrug, trying to ignore the butterflies in my stomach. Who knew ghosts could be so attractive? "I am a paranormal YouTuber. Love love love the paranormal. Obsessed. Plus, you're not exactly the scariest ghost I've ever seen," I pause to admire his chest. "Nice muscles, by the way."

Ethan's eyes widen, and if ghosts could blush, I swear he would be. "I... what?"

"You heard me," I say, winking. "Now, since we're going to be roomies, want to help me unpack? I've got an Ouija board in one of these boxes – we could have a proper chat."

Ethan's form flickers, and for a moment, I think he might disappear. But then he solidifies again, a reluctant smile tugging at his lips. "LEAVE."

"Nope," I say, popping the 'p.' "You're stuck with me, hot stuff. Might as well make the best of it."

I return to my unpacking, humming again. Ethan moves to stand beside me, a cool breeze. "What's an Ouija board?" his voice growing stronger.

· · ·

I laugh, shaking my head. "Oh, Ethan, we have so much to talk about."

DATE NIGHT

ETHAN

I materialize in Chloe's bedroom, hovering over her. My spectral hands reach toward her as I let out a bone-chilling moan. Chloe's eyes flutter open. She yawns and stretches, completely unfazed.

"Good morning to you too, Casper," she smirks. "Trying the whole 'scare the mortal' bit again? How original."

I recoil, scowling. "I am not Casper. I am Ethan, the terrifying ghost who haunts this house." Did I really just say that?

Chloe sits up and looks straight at me, her green eyes sparkling with amusement. Her hand runs through the messy brown curls. So sexy. "Oh, I'm absolutely quaking. Look at me, trembling." She wiggles her long, pale fingers mockingly.

She is infuriating.

. . .

"You know," Chloe continues, "for a ghost, you're not very good at the whole scaring thingy. Maybe try taking some classes? I hear there's a seminar next week - 'Haunting 101: How to Terrify Mortals in 3 Easy Steps.'"

Woman, if you don't stop, I am going to spank you. Her tank top has slipped off one shoulder, revealing smooth, velvety skin. No, focus. I'm here to scare her, not ogle her. Although ... she has the most glorious round breasts I have ever seen ... and I have seen a lot.

"You'll regret moving into this house," I growl. "I'll make your life a living hell."

Chloe yawns again. "Mhm. Coffee first, hellish torment later. Coming downstairs?"

Before I can respond, she's padding out of the room toward the kitchen. I float after her, fuming. I summon my energy and fly the cabinets open, rattle the dishes and turn on the faucet full blast, with water spraying everywhere. The lights flicker wildly. Chloe calmly sidesteps the chaos, grabbing a mug from the open cabinet. "Thanks for that," she says. "I couldn't reach the top shelf."

My jaw drops. Is she serious? "Are you serious?"

. . .

She shrugs, filling the filter. "What can I say? I'm a 'glass half full' gal—in this case, mug half full—of delicious coffee."

I float closer, looming over her. "I could destroy you with a thought."

Chloe churns, looking up at me with those sparkling eyes. "You're such a drama queen."

"I am the very embodiment of evil!"I sputter. How dare she?

"Uh-huh, scary ..." clearly not buying it. "And I'm the Queen of England. Do you want coffee or not?"

"I... what? I'm a ghost. I can't drink coffee."

"Suit yourself, " she shrugs. "More for me." She bustles around the kitchen, humming softly. I find myself oddly mesmerized. Her complete lack of fear is infuriating, yes, but also... intriguing. I've never met anyone like her in all my years haunting this house. Or ever.

"Tell me about yourself, Ethan," Chloe says, settling at the kitchen table with her steaming mug. "How did you end up haunting this place?"

"What?"I scoff.

. . .

"Oh, I see, being mysterious, " she grins. "Let me guess - spurned lover? Betrayed by your best friend? Killed in a freak accident involving a toaster and a rubber duck?"

"You have quite the imagination." I'm trying, I am really trying to resist, but I feel the corners of my mouth twitching despite myself. She winks and smiles. Her pink tongue peaks through and I want to devour her. I wonder how would it feel, to taste her. Can I ?

Days go by, and each day, I find it increasingly difficult to keep up the facade. Chloe treats me more like an amusing roommate. Witty banter, quips back and forth. She chats with me while doing chores and even leaves the TV on when she goes out to keep me company. It's infuriating. And oddly... nice. But I want more.

One evening, I'm sulking in the attic, brooding over her, when I hear voices downstairs. I can't believe it! My non-existent heart plummets at the sight before me. Chloe is laughing and chatting with someone I've never seen before. A man! He's tall, handsome, well, kind of, if you like that sort of thing, and very much alive.

"This is such a cool place," he says, looking around.

Chloe grins. "Oh, you have no idea. Sometimes it feels like it's straight out of a horror movie." How dare she bring a man into our home? Doesn't she know she belongs to me now?

"Very cool. Perfect for Halloween." Cool? Is that the only word he knows? I show you cool. I start with the light first, flickering. Then a cold wind through the room, rattling the windows and the TV turning off and on by itself, blaring static.

The man looks around nervously. "Uh, is that normal?"

But Chloe just laughs, "Oh, don't worry. It's all part of the Halloween atmosphere I set up. Pretty realistic, huh?" I swear I can see her sending me a menacing glance. Her lips purse. "STOP IT!"

I watch them set up on the couch and continue the date. How can she act so nonchalant? Can't she see how wrong this is? She is mine.I cause every book to fly off the shelves, swirling around the room like a literary tornado.

"Oh, wow!" Chloe starts clapping her hands. "I didn't think the special effects would work this well. Isn't it amazing? Do you like it?"

Do you like it??!

. . .

"This is incredible," the idiot says, looking impressed. "How did you set all this up?"

"It's a secret," she winks. "Now, how about some dinner? I make a mean pumpkin risotto." Wink now?

I drift after them, watching as Chloe effortlessly weaves my supernatural outbursts into her Halloween-themed night. Every rattling cabin becomes a spooky sound effect, and every flickering light is mood lighting. She's turned my haunting into a romantic ambiance. Damn her.

As I watch them enjoy their meal, laughing and flirting, an unfamiliar ache settles in my spectral chest. I want her—her laughter, her wit, her fearless spirit. Her tits. Her juicy mouth. That gorgeous ass.

For the first time in decades, I wish I was alive again.

ALMOST KISSED

CHLOE

The candlelight casts shadows across Mark's face as he leans in. My heart is pounding, but not from excitement—from dread. I know what's coming, and I know it won't end well. A blast of freezing air sweeps through the room just as Mark's lips are about to touch mine.

"What the fuck?" Mark jerks back, eyes wide.

A deep, scary growl reverberates through the house, seeming to come from everywhere and nowhere at once.

"It's probably just the wind." I say weakly, knowing full well it isn't. Damn it, Ethan. The lights begin to flash erratically, and objects start flying off shelves. A heavy book narrowly misses Mark's head.

. . .

"I need to get out of here!" Mark shouts, already backing toward the door. "I'll call you!" Yeah, right.

I want to tell him to stay, to explain, but I know it's pointless. "I'm so sorry," I call after him as he bolts.

Once the front door slams shut, fury bubbles up inside me. "Ethan!" I yell. "Show yourself, RIGHT NOW!"

He materializes before me, looking infuriatingly handsome and completely unrepentant. So close. So far.

"You, you ... asshole!"

"He's not good enough for you," Ethan blurts out.

"That's none of your business! Why do you care?"

"Don't you know?" He's now even closer, his eyes fixed on mine. "You are mine!" The words blast out from him.

My mind is spinning. He reaches for me, but his hand passes right through my arm. Frustration flashes across his face as he tries again, managing only to create a tingling sensation where his fingers should be.

· · ·

"It's okay," I whisper, even though it's not. Nothing about this is okay.

Ethan leans in, his lips hovering just above mine. I close my eyes in anticipation. My heart is pounding. God, I have been wanting this! But all I feel is a cool whisper of air.

When I open my eyes, Ethan looks devastated. "I want you so badly," he says softly.

"I know," I reply, surprised to find I'm fighting back tears. "I want you too."

WHATEVER HAPPENS

ETHAN

D amn it. I try to touch her but she is slipping right through my fingers. I want her. I need her. Shit, I LOVE her. Love. A new thing for me.

My skin tingles, "What is happening?" I can feel the distance between worlds thinning. "My hands ..." The clock strikes midnight. I look down and see solid flesh, whereas only mist existed.

There's so much I want to say, but that can wait. I pull her to me and press my lips to hers. I wanted to taste her for so long. She melts against me with a soft moan that ignites my blood. My body responds and I feel myself growing hard. I missed THAT. My hands roam possessively over her curves now as I back her up against the wall.

"You're mine," I growl between kisses. I want more.

. . .

"Oh God, Yes," Chloe breathes. Her hands go around my neck, and her kisses deepen. I pinch her nipples through the soft fabric of the dress. "Mmm, Ethan ... " she moans softly. Heck. I rip it off, eager to see and take those large puppies in my mouth. I circle my tongue and suck them hard, one hand sliding between her thighs. She is wet for me already. I go down and lick and nib between her fold, two fingers pumping in and out of her. I work her hard until I feel her throbbing.

"E..e...t...h..AAAAN," her body jerks, and she comes in my hand. "That was nice."

"Baby, that was just the appetizer." I lift her up and carry her to the bedroom. I pause for a minute to take her all in. Her eyes go wide as my cock stands for attention. With a groan, I position myself at her entrance and slowly push inside her warmth. Her walls clench around me, hot and wet. When I feel she is ready, I push forward slowly, then hard and fast.

"Ethan," she moans my name like a prayer and I almost lose it. "Yes, right there." Her legs are all around me, calling me in, and I pound in and out, thrusting hard.

"You are mine now."

"I'm yours."

· · ·

"No other," I order, "Say it."

"No other, I...I..."

Her nails score my back as she climaxes with a cry, and I follow her over the edge, spilling myself within her.

Whatever happens, we are joined now, the two of us.

EPILOGUE
CHLOE

I rest my hand on my swollen belly and I can feel a gentle kick. Ethan's reflection appears behind me as I look to the ornate Victorian mirror we restored last month. His arms wrap tight around my waist.

"Are you ready for the ghost tour, my beautiful medium?" his breath is warm against my ear.

I lean back into his solid chest, marveling at how real he feels. "Always ready to terrify the tourists, my handsome specter."

Ethan chuckles, spinning me to face him. "I'm hardly spectral anymore, thanks to you."

"Oh please," I retort, straightening his jacket. "You're still as otherworldly as the day I moved in."

· · ·

"Who knew 'The Hot Ghost' would be so successful?" I continue, "the start to all this ... "

"Who wouldn't want to read about a devastatingly attractive ghost and the beautiful mortal who steals his heart?" he replies. "Obvious best seller material!"

"Modest as usual, I see." God, he makes me laugh.

"Shall I give them a real fright tonight?" His eyes sparkle with mischief. "Perhaps I could walk through a wall for old times' sake?"

"And risk giving someone a fainting spell?" I slap his arm playfully. "I think not. Besides, the baby doesn't appreciate your ghostly antics."

As if on cue, another kick. Ethan's hand joins mine; his touch is reverent. "Our little phantom," he whispers.

I roll my eyes but can't suppress a grin. "This child will be impossibly dramatic with you as a father."

Ethan smiles. "Takes after its mother, I'd wager."

As we descend the grand staircase, I take in the sight of our beautifully restored home. The antique wallpaper, the polished wood, the flickering gas lamps—a portal to another time.

"Do you ever regret.." I ask softly. "being... you know... mo..."

"Sssh," Ethan whispers and then turns serious, cupping my face in his hands.

"Chloe, my love, I wouldn't trade this life with you for anything."

The doorbell chimes, "They are here," tonight's tour group has arrived. I break away reluctantly, smoothing my dress.

"Showtime," I announce with a grin. "Ready to make some believers?"

"After you." Ethan offers his arm with a flourish and then disappears.

Together, we open the door to welcome a new group of wide-eyed visitors eager to share our extraordinary home's magic and mystery—and an even more extraordinary love story. Ours.

THE BAD SAINT

PROLOGUE

LUKE

I stare into the fire crackling in the stone hearth, flames licking over logs, shadows dancing across the walls of my cabin. It's the only noise that makes sense to me anymore, the only one that doesn't feel like static buzzing through my skull, needling at me, scratching old wounds. The headlines flash before my eyes, even now. "Local Hero Saves Dozens in Tragic Fire." My stomach churns at the memory.

They called me The Saint. Me—a guy who got a few people out of a burning building by doing what anyone would've done if they had the guts to risk it. But that's what makes it sting, I guess. Because deep down, I know not everyone would've done what I did. And maybe I shouldn't have.

People in Cedar Pines like their heroes simple. They need the cardboard cutout, the local golden boy who's shiny clean and dependable. A hero who'll throw himself into a building with flames roaring from every window and come out with a kid tucked under each arm, never thinking twice. They needed someone to look up to, to believe in. I gave them that once, and I hated every damn second of it. Not that anyone cared to notice.

They sure as hell didn't see what it cost me. The whiskey bottle beckons from the kitchen counter. A familiar call. I pour a glass, hands shaking, and down it in one burning gulp. "To Saint Luke," I raise the empty glass in a mock toast. The irony twists like a knife. Black smoke, heat pressing down on me until my lungs felt like they'd collapse. I hear sound of screaming, voices of people I barely knew, faces I can't remember, and the overwhelming silence after it was all over. They don't know the sound of flesh burning, don't know what it does to you when you smell it on your skin. And that was before my world cracked apart, and I lost the one person who ever made this life make sense. Sarah. My wife. Gone in an instant while I was off playing savior.

I grip the counter, squeezing my eyes shut. I take deep breaths—in and out. The flashback fades, leaving me drained.

I go back in my leather armchair, feeling the weight settle over me again. I've been living out here, surrounded by trees and silence, for years, and they still whisper about it. I try not to give them any reason to remember me. Keep to myself. Stock up on groceries once a month, avoid eye contact. Let the rumors spin however they want.

Because I'm not that man anymore. I rub a hand over my jaw, feeling the scratch of stubble. My reflection stares back from the window, a shadowed figure with too many scars. The man looking back at me isn't a hero, and he sure as hell isn't a saint.

THE ARRIVAL

AVA

I clutch the steering wheel as I turn onto a barely visible gravel road, every tree closing in like nature itself wants to keep me out. Cedar Pines locals call this road a "path." I call it an obstacle course. The closer I get, the more my pulse picks up. This is the big break I've been waiting for—a chance to interview *the* Luke Warren, a man who hasn't been seen in town since he saved half of it from burning to the ground.

People around here talk about him like he's a legend, some sort of mythical creature. The Saint. But from the reports I've read and the vague quotes I've managed to wring out of people, he sounds more like a ghost—a man they loved, then lost and aren't sure they'd even recognize anymore. Hell, he doesn't even go by Luke Warren in the town records. Just Luke. Like some mystery out of an old western.

The cabin finally comes into view, tucked back in a small clearing. It's far from dilapidated, though—more like rugged, with a dark cedar exterior, sturdy porch, and enough land around it to make it clear he doesn't want visitors. But I didn't drive out here on this glorified goat path just to turn around at the sight of a well-built house. I'm getting my interview, even if I have to camp out here until he gives in.

I park my car and take a deep breath. The winter air bites into my cheeks as I step out. I smooth down my coat, acutely aware of how it clings to my curves. Perhaps I should have worn something warmer and less fancy. I barely have time to look around before the door swings open, and *he* steps out.

"Hmmm," I'm lost for words, which isn't like me. But then again, Luke Warren isn't like anyone. Tall, built like he could swing an ax through a tree in one swing, arms thick and muscular. A glimpse of tattoos that snake down his wrists. Nothing like the clean-cut hero I remember from news footage. There's this dark edge to him, something that almost vibrates off his skin. A warning impossible to ignore. But it's his face that stops me cold: strong, rough, with a square jaw dusted with stubble and eyes the color of a storm.

I realize I'm staring. And worse, he's staring right back, those dark eyes narrowing like he's sizing me up and finding me wanting.

"Whatever you're selling, I'm not interested," he says, voice low and gravelly. "You can turn around and head back to town."

I clear my throat, feeling a bit of heat creeping into my cheeks. Pull it together, Ava. "I'm... I'm not selling anything. My name is Ava Sinclair. I'm a journalist with The Cedar Chronicle, and I'm here to interview you about the disaster. The town's holding a memorial and I thought people would like to hear from the man who saved half of them."

"Yeah? Well, the town can keep their memorial and the newspaper too," he mutters, already turning back to the door.

"Please, just five minutes of your time. The ten-year anniversary—"

"I said no."

My stomach tightens, but I can't let this slip away. I take a step forward, planting myself in his line of sight. "It's been years since you spoke to anyone about it. People look up to you, you know? They call you The Saint."

Something dark flits across his face at that name, and his jaw sets, the hard line of it making my chest tighten in a way that's not entirely professional. Heck, he is hot. He glares at me, but I hold my ground as he steps closer, his presence filling up every inch of air between us.

"I didn't ask to be called that," he growls. "And I didn't ask for you to show up on my doorstep like some—"

"Some what? Persistent journalist trying to do her job?" I fire back, my hands on my hips. "Look, I'm not here to annoy you. I'm here to do my job and maybe to remind you that people care about what you did. That they still look up to you."

He barks out a laugh, but there's no humor in it. "You really think a few nice words from me will make them feel better about their lives?"

"It might. Or maybe it's just about closure. Letting people know you're OK."

He's quiet for a long moment. Those stormy eyes still locked on me. Finally, he mutters something under his breath, and his expression changes, softening just a fraction. "Five minutes, that's it."

Victory. I suppress a smile and step past him into the cabin, acutely aware of his eyes fixed on me as I walk in. I can't help but feel a surge of triumph—and something else. Something I absolutely refuse to acknowledge. The interior is cozy, more than I expected—a mix of leather furniture, book-shelves stacked with worn novels, and a big stone fireplace crackling with warmth. It's rugged but well-kept, and I can't help but feel like it's… him.

He closes the door behind us and folds his arms, watching me with that unreadable look. "Ask your questions and be done with it."

I nod, pulling my notepad from my bag. My fingers feel clumsy, my mind racing to stay focused when he's so… close and so much man all at once. I clear my throat, glancing up at him. "When you look back on that day, what do you think?"

Luke's eyes narrow. "I don't look back on it. That's the point."

"Well, if you could say one thing to the people you helped that day, what would it be?"

"Nothing," he replies, his tone clipped. "There's nothing to say."

I can feel him retreating, emotionally barricading himself and frustration surging up inside me. "There's gotta be something. People look at you like some... untouchable hero. Well, The Saint. Don't you want them to know you're human?"

"Don't call me that." His eyes flash dangerously, hands balling into fists. "They don't need to know a damn thing about me, least of all you." He steps closer, and I can feel the heat rolling off him. His anger. Underneath it, a magnetic pull that's making it hard to breathe.

I hold up my hands. "Sorry, I just— Maybe they just need you," I add quickly. His face softens a little when he hears that and his eyes drop to my mouth. I feel a heat ripple between us, my heart is pounding. Then he blinks, and the walls slam back up.

"We're done here. Find someone else to be your hero." He jerks open the door and kind of shoves me outside.

What just happened? All I know is I'm not done with him —not yet.

YOU AGAIN?

AVA

I make my way back to the cabin the next morning, my breath puffing out in little clouds. I can practically feel the bite of his dismissive tone —sharp, abrasive, meant to drive me away. It would've worked on someone else. I'm not someone else.

I didn't drive three hours and put up with his towering attitude just to turn tail because he's grouchy.

The cabin looms ahead, dark and solid against the morning light. I notice an old truck parked out front this time, its body caked in mud but gleaming under a fresh layer of frost. I wonder what Luke's like behind the wheel of it, probably driving fast with his jaw set in that hard line, all while cranking rock music to match his mood. For a split second, I can picture it so clearly that my heart does an odd little jump. OK, a big jump.

Shaking it off I step onto his porch, summoning every ounce of confidence as I knock. The door swings open almost immediately, and Luke fills the doorway, broad shoulders crowding the space as if he's physically blocking me from entering his world. His face is carved from stone, his eyes a shade darker than yesterday, if that's even possible.

"You again?" His voice is low as if he's already two seconds away from losing his patience.

"Good morning to you too." I let my mouth curve up just enough to make it clear I'm not backing down.

His eyes narrow, the faintest hint of irritation ticking in his jaw. "You've got guts, I'll give you that. But I thought I made myself clear. I'm not interested."

I cross my arms, mirroring his stance. "Not even if I'm the only one who can make it look good? Besides, we barely scratched the surface yesterday. I drove all this way; the least you could do is offer me a cup of coffee."

Luke's eyes flicker, and I swear, for half a second, there's something almost amused there. But then he grunts, stepping back just enough to let me through. I take whatever this is. I can feel him every step I take but, when I glance over my shoulder, he's just watching, a hint of exasperation darkening his eyes.

Inside, the cabin is still warm from the fire crackling in the stone hearth. The scent of coffee permeates the air.

"I'm not offering any coffee," he says flatly, breaking the silence. "You want to talk, talk. But make it quick." Charming.

I perch on the edge of the couch, crossing my legs slowly, letting him see that I'm here to stay. "Fine. Yesterday, you said you don't look back on what happened. But if you're really that indifferent, why are you hiding out here instead of living your life?"

He crosses his arms on his chest and leans back against the counter, his expression as closed off as a vault. "Hiding? That what you think I'm doing?"

"Seems pretty obvious," I say, shrugging like it's the most casual observation in the world. "The Saint disappears right after the big rescue and goes into full isolation mode. What other conclusion am I supposed to draw?"

His eyes flash, something dark and molten simmering beneath the surface. I shouldn't have called him that again.

"You're assuming a lot for someone who doesn't know the first damn thing about me."

"Then tell me." I lean forward, eyes steady on his. "Tell me what made you leave. Tell me why you won't even step foot back in Cedar Pines, why people only ever talk about you in the past tense."

Silence thickens between us, air heavy, but he doesn't break eye contact. "If you come out here looking for heroes and happy endings, you're in the wrong place."

I refuse to let his words sting me. "I'm not looking for a hero. I just want to tell a story. And if you were really as hardened as you want me to believe, you wouldn't be this rattled by me digging."

"Rattled?" His lips twitch in a dangerous sort of smile. "Sweetheart, I'm not rattled."

"Ava," I correct sharply. He pushes off from the counter and takes a few slow, measured steps closer. My heart picks up speed. I hold my ground, trying to ignore the wave of heat coursing through me at his nearness.

"Why are you really here?" His voice is low, almost intimate, like a whisper. I can feel it down to my bones. "Because I don't buy for a second that it's just for the anniversary."

"I don't know, maybe I'm just curious about the big, bad Saint who shut himself off from the world," I say, my voice steady, even as my pulse betrays me. "And maybe I'm not someone who runs when things get difficult."

He lets out a dry laugh, looking away like he's trying to contain himself. His eyes then drop to my lips, then back to my eyes, heat simmering. For a heartbeat, I think he might kiss me. "Curiosity killed the cat, Sinclair."

Why doesn't he say my name?

Before I can respond, my phone buzzes in my pocket and breaks the spell. I glance at the screen. Luke looks down and something darkens in his expression.

"You got someone waiting on you?" he asks, voice clipped, eyes trained on my phone like it's an intruder.

I frown, taken aback by the sudden edge in his tone. "My editor! Is that a problem?"

"Sure it was," a flash of jealousy, hot and unmistakably possessive, but he quickly schools his face back to indifference. A tiny crack in the armor. Part of me wants to slap that look off his face. Another part... "You know, for someone so determined to stay isolated, you're awfully invested in my personal life."

"I'm not," he snorts, stepping back as if to put a barrier between us. "You don't belong here."

"Maybe I don't. But you know what? You don't either, Mr Saint. You're hiding because it's easier than facing the truth."

He pauses, shoulders tensed, moving back closer "And what truth is that?" He is awfully deliciously close.

"That maybe YOU need saving." The words slip out, soft but bold, and for a second, he's frozen.

THE STORM

LUKE

The wind is howling, and the sky's gone dark. I can see the storm rolling in. I've already checked the windows and brought in the wood, doing my best to ignore the fact that I've got this stubborn, annoyingly sexy reporter sitting on my couch who doesn't seem to know when to quit or leave.

I glance over watching her fight with the old quilt she's wrapped around her shoulders, trying to warm up. Her thin coat barely conceals her gorgeous curves. A city coat. The storm is picking up so fast that there's no chance of her returning to town tonight. She's stuck here, and so am I. My body knows it before my head does. I can feel her, every inch of her, right there on my couch, like she's invaded more than just my space—like she's waltzed straight into the parts of me I'd locked down a long time ago.

Need saving, she says...

"A storm is coming," I say before I lose myself. The fireplace crackles between us, casting her in a soft, flickering light that's doing things to me I've got no business feeling. "Guess you're stuck here until morning."

She looks up, an unreadable expression as she raises an

eyebrow. "Guess I am. Hope you're not about to tell me I'm cramping your style."

"Cramping?" I say crossing my arms over my chest as I lean against the doorframe. "You could say that. But it's more the headache you're giving me that's getting on my nerves."

Her mouth quirks up, and she tosses the quilt aside, sitting up straighter like she's daring me to get closer. "I can always grab my things and drive back to town. I'm sure I can manage."

I shake my head. "You'd be lost and then I'll have to come and rescue you."

"You'd like that," she says and folds her arms, framing her round breasts. I see the faintest shiver run through her. She's got a fire in her that turns me on, even if it's making this whole situation far more dangerous than I want it to be. My cock is pulsing.

"Fine," she continues, "then how about you stop brooding and be a decent host?" And then she lifts her chin in a way that makes me want to kiss her. Hard. Make her mine.

But that's not happening. Not in a million years. I walk over to the window to check the shutters, trying to keep my hands busy. "Need me to grab you anything?"

She doesn't respond, but I can feel her eyes on my back, intense enough to make the hairs on my neck stand up. I don't turn around. Not until she sighs and drops her arms, letting a flicker of vulnerability show.

"You're a mystery, Luke Warren," she says softly. "I wonder if anyone has ever gotten close enough to know the real you."

I let out a dry laugh, but the bitterness is obvious, even to my ears. "Maybe that's the point. Maybe I don't want anyone close enough."

She doesn't flinch, and for a second, I almost wish she would. I want her to stop staring at me. But she doesn't move. She just watches me, her eyes steady, challenging. She's too damn close—emotionally, physically—and there's not enough air in this room to keep my walls up.

"If you don't want anyone close, then why am I still here?" she whispers, her voice barely audible over the crackling fire.

Damn her. "Beside the storm?" I step closer without realizing it until I'm just a few feet away. "You're here because you're too damn stubborn to take a hint," I say, voice rough. I can feel her warmth. Soo close.

She laughs softly, almost like she's enjoying this too much. "And here I thought you were supposed to be a saint. What happened to that?"

I don't know if it's the confined space, the isolation or the way her voice has dropped to a tone that makes me feel like I'm about to unravel, but something inside me snaps. I move toward her, stepping over to the couch until I'm towering over her, my fists clenched at my sides. "What happened? Life happened. The real world isn't some fairy tale. It breaks you if you let it, and there's no one coming around to fix what's left."

Her lips part, but she doesn't look afraid. If anything, there's something...soft , something that reaches straight through my anger and wraps around the broken parts of me. And I hate it. I hate that she's here, seeing this, but I can't turn away.

She reaches up, tentatively placing a hand on my arm, and the touch is like fire. I grab her wrist. "You don't get it," I rasp, my voice raw. "You don't want this."

She leans in and the whole world goes silent, leaving only the sound of our breathing. "Maybe I do, Luke." My name on her lips ...Before I know it, my mouth is on hers, claiming her with a hunger I've been holding back since I saw her. Her lips are soft and yielding, and when she puts her arms around my neck, pulling me closer, I lose the last bit of control I had. I kiss her like a man who's been starved, pouring every ounce of frustration and need into it. She tastes like heaven. Our bodies press together and I guide her back until she's lying beneath me, looking up at me with eyes so full of trust it hurts. "Are you sure?" I rasp, my hands trembling as I brush the hair from her face.

She smiles and reaches up to pull me down, her answer clear without words.

Her nails dig into my shoulders, her breath hot against my skin. My hands roam her curves, desperate to touch every inch of her. Ava moans, the sound driving me wild. I pant as I trail kisses down her neck. I stop to drink in the sight of her. Hair tousled, lips swollen, chest heaving. "Are you sure?" I ask again hoarsely. "Please," Ava begs. " I want you." I rip her clothes off her and worship every inch of her silky skin with my hands and mouth. She whispers my name, each sound drawing me deeper, closer until there's nothing left but the feeling of her beneath me, soft and warm and mine.

I tease her entry with my fingers while I suck her hardened nipples. One finger, two fingers, three fingers… "Oh, this is nice," she says. She reaches out and gently runs her hand up and down my thick length. God, that's fucking hot. I can feel her pussy tightening around my fingers when I pull away. "I want to lick you," I say as I put her legs over my shoulders. " I've been dying to do this." Ava groans and moans at my first lick and nip. Fingers and tongue, fingers and tongue. Her pussy smells so good, tastes so sweet. Sweet enough to eat. I nibble at her clit, my fingers pounding. Her hips move with every thrust.

"YEEEEES,' she screams. "More… more…" I can't wait any longer. I plunge my cock into her warm wet pussy, hard and fast. I seize her hips and lift her lower half off the couch completely and pound. Wildly. It doesn't take long before she cries out her release and I fall right behind her. I close my eyes and just breathe.

"What happens now?" She looks up at me with a sleepy smile that threatens to undo me all over again.

I know there's no answer I can give that won't tear this moment apart. I've crossed a line I swore I'd never cross. Let someone in when I vowed I'd never again. But I know one thing: I can't let go of this, whatever it is.

CRAZY CITY GIRL

AVA

The morning light filters through the curtains, waking me up. I forget where I am for a second until the ache in my body reminds me—a deep, raw ache from last night.

Memories flood back. The heat in his eyes, the way he looked at me like he'd been starving, the rough urgency of his touch. Luke has a darkness about him, and it poured into every second of what we shared. Yet, here I am, still craving him. Maybe even more.

But his side of the bed is empty. I sit up, pulling the sheets to my chest as I scan the room. My heart stumbles a little. Part of me wants to curl up, savor the ache and pretend last night was the whole story. But I know it's not. And I think I know enough of him to realize he won't make it easy to untangle whatever happened between us.

I wrap myself in Luke's discarded jumper and pad downstairs. I find him outside, leaning against the railing of the porch, hands stuffed into his pockets as he stares out into the woods. He doesn't acknowledge me as I step out, but I know he hears me. I stop just a few feet behind him, crossing my arms.

"You left before I woke up," I say, my voice still scratchy.

He doesn't turn. "Didn't think you'd want to see me first thing in the morning."

I take a deep breath. This man. He's so close that he can't even see how much last night meant to me—how much HE means to me.

"Luke," I start, stepping forward, trying to find the words. "You know, most people around here still think of you as a hero."

He lets out a low, humorless chuckle, his head dropping forward. "A hero. That's what they call people who can barely sleep through the night without getting haunted by their damn memories?"

I close the distance between us until I'm right beside him, leaning on the railing. I wait a beat, gathering my words. "You saved lives, Luke. A lot of lives. And just because you're hurting doesn't mean it's any less true."

He scoffs and finally turns to look at me. Sharp, defensive, angry. But beneath it, I see the hurt. "You have no idea, Ava. No idea what it was like. The things ... the things I couldn't stop…people I couldn't save… people I lost."

I grab his arm, feeling the tension thrumming beneath his skin. "Then tell me. Let me in."

His jaw clenches, and he shakes his head, his mouth bitterly twisting. "Why? For your story?"

"Seriously? After last night you are asking me that?" I snap, losing my patience.

He pulls back, scrubbing a hand over his face. Is he going to walk away?

"I've never talked about it," he says quietly.

I move closer and lay a hand on his chest, "Then tell me."

And finally, he does. Slowly, his voice rough and raw, he tells me about the smoke, the heat. How he fought until his body couldn't take it, until he was half-dead himself. And then the guilt, the pain, the nightmares that never left him. The wife that left him when he was at his most vulnerable. By the end, his voice is a rasp, his shoulders hunched like he's trying to shrink from his memories. I reach up, cupping his face in my hands, forcing him to look at me. "Luke, listen to me. You don't have to be perfect. You just have to be you. No one expected you to save everyone. Sometimes...just being there is enough."

He swallows hard. "Why do you bother?" he whispers, almost to himself.

I smile a little, running my thumb over his jaw, feeling the roughness of his stubble. "Because I care, you idiot."

Something breaks in his eyes. He dips his head, his mouth brushing mine so softly it makes my breath hitch. "I don't deserve you," he murmurs. His hands slide to my waist, pulling me against him as if he can't help himself. "But I'm done pretending I don't want you. Need you."

And then his mouth is on mine again. But this time it's different, softer, no anger, no frustration—only a deep, aching need. His hands trace all over my body with a reverence that nearly breaks my heart. I feel his breath against my neck. I hold him closer, letting him feel that I'm here—that I'm not going anywhere.

"Crazy city girl," he says as he wraps his coat around me. "You are shivering." And then pulls me over his shoulder and carries me inside.

In the quiet morning light, he makes love to me again, but this time it's slow and tender like he's pouring every unspoken word into each touch and kiss. And I can feel it— the depth of his emotions, the love he has inside. When he finally whispers my name, it's like a promise, a vow I feel down to my bones.

Afterward, we lie together. I rest my head on his chest, and he strokes my hair, his fingers gentle, as if he's afraid I'll disappear.

"You know you're mine now, right?" he says softly, but there's a possessive edge to his voice that sends a thrill through me. "And I'm yours. If you'll have me."

"I love you," he whispers against my skin. "I think I have from the moment I saw you."

Tears prick my eyes. "I love you too," I breathe.

EPILOGUE
LUKE

The morning sun glints off the polished granite of the memorial, and I close my eyes for a second. Ava's hand is warm in mine, steady as hell. I breathe deeply, letting the cool breeze settle the nerves rumbling in my gut. But when I open my eyes, a wall of faces staring back at me, a mix of shock, curiosity, and maybe a little hope. I watch a ripple run through the crowd. They're looking at me like I'm a ghost from the past, like they're seeing the guy who used to be ready to save the world. But I'm not that guy anymore, and for once in my life, I'm alright with that.

"Is that…is that really him?" someone whispers, voice low but clear enough to cut through the silence around us. Ava's fingers give mine a quick squeeze, grounding me, anchoring me.

The mayor steps up and clears his throat before addressing everyone. "Today, we remember those we lost and honor those who risked everything to save others."

A familiar tightness presses down on my chest. But this time, it's different. It's bearable. I look down at Ava, at the strength in her eyes, and she murmurs, "You okay?"

"Yeah," I reply, voice low. "I am now."

The ceremony goes on, but I barely hear it. Memories flicker in and out like an old film reel, each hitting a little softer with her beside me. She's the only damn thing I need.

When it's all over, an elderly man steps up to us, eyes full of tears. "Thank you," he whispers, grabbing my hand with a grip surprisingly strong for someone his age. "For everything you did that day."

I swallow hard, nodding. "I just wish I could've done more."

We turn to leave, and with Ava's hand still locked in mine, I feel the weight I've carried for years begin to lift. The burden slips off my shoulders. I'm here. I'm healing. And I've got someone to hold onto.

"You ready to go home?" Ava asks, her gaze soft, full of that love she somehow has for me.

"With you?" I ask, voice low, warmth filling me in a way I almost forgot was possible. "Always."

As we step through the crowd, I slide my arm around her waist, fingers splayed across her hip in a way that says she's mine. She laughs, low and soft, "You know, they're all staring, right?"

"Let them." I pull her in closer, smirk tugging at my mouth. "I want everyone to know you're mine."

She turns to look at me, her eyes so damn soft I feel it like a punch. "And you're mine."

"I love you, Ava," I whisper, the words rolling out easy, like they were always meant to be said. "How about we make this official?"

"Luke Warren, are you asking me..."

"I am ... mine, till death do us part."

THE FALLEN HERO

GHOSTS OF US

COLE

I tell myself to just breathe. In. Out. Simple. But standing here on this quiet stretch of road leading back to town, it's not simple. It's the hardest damn thing I've done since…well, since I made the kind of choice a man's supposed to be able to live with. The kind I couldn't.

Two years. That's how long I've been gone. I shouldn't even be here now, but some things feel… unavoidable. Maybe that's what this is—a mission I can't refuse. Honor the fallen. Face the whispers, the sideways looks. But I know it's more than that, and it sure as hell isn't just about honor.

It's about Emma.

It's about her and everything we had before I left. Everything we could've been if I hadn't walked away without looking back, my eyes fixed ahead as if she wasn't standing there, shattered, watching me disappear. Just the thought of her name hits me like a shot of whiskey, burning and warm, settling in a place I can't quite reach. I didn't expect her to still haunt me after all this time, but she does. It's a strange kind of torture, the one you keep coming back to like an old habit.

I've kept tabs on her. I don't even try to pretend I haven't. Every once in a while, I'll look her up, see her smile on some town event flyer, hear her voice on a voicemail I'll never answer. Selfish, maybe, but I had to know. She hasn't moved on, at least not like I thought she would. Not like she deserves. And here I am, hoping the town forgot about me... while I remember every damn thing about her.

The memory of her face—soft, sweet, and just as angry as she was heartbroken—is still burned in my mind. It was the last thing I saw before I turned my back.

I should turn around now, too. Get back in my truck and disappear. Spare her from seeing me again, from reopening scars. I was the one who left. I should go, but my feet won't move. Instead, my eyes lock on the town's silhouette in the morning fog, and all I can think about is Emma. Her laugh, her warmth, the way she could make this place feel like home. And for the first time in a long time, I realize...I want it back.

Only question is...does she?

THE RETURN

EMMA

The clink clink clink of mugs and the hum hum humming of early morning conversations wash over me as I run a rag over the café counter. This place is as much a part of me as the ache in my chest. The one that settled in when Cole left and never fully went away.

Two years. Two years of trying to forget, of telling myself that if he didn't need me, I didn't need him.

And now I've heard he's back. The whisper reached me this morning. "Did you hear? Cole... He is back!" I thought I was ready for this—God, I've had two years to get ready. But hearing his name still makes my stomach twist.

I thought I hated him for leaving. For disappearing without a word. I spent months crying, then I spent months furious. And yet, here I am, two years later, still haunted. The way he used to pull me in close, so close that everything else just faded away. It was real...at least, I thought it was.

I sigh, straightening the row of napkins by the register, anything to keep my hands busy. Because here's the truth: if he's back in town, it's only a matter of time before I see him again. And ...what then? Do I act like he doesn't still own every damn piece of my heart? Do I let him see that he broke it?

I'm stronger now, or at least I want to be. And if I see him, I'll be ready. I'll tell him he doesn't get to waltz back into my life. That he made his choice, and I moved on. But the thought of that moment, of facing him again, of feeling his eyes on me...

I'm terrified that if he walks back in, I won't be able to let him go a second time.

REMEMBRANCE

COLE

Returning to Haverhill feels like waking from a long, dark sleep. The familiar streets, the brick facades of old mill buildings, even the stubborn New England trees—all of it rushes at me with a force that's almost physical. The town looks smaller than I remember. Or maybe I'm the one who's changed, worn down, and stripped bare over the years. I park the truck and kill the engine, letting the silence settle. The town square is already filling with people, a sea of red, white, and blue. Kids with pinwheels, veterans in faded uniforms, and families with lawn chairs and coolers. A banner stretches across Main Street: "Remember Our Heroes."

The war's over at least the one on paper. The real battle—the one lodged inside my skull—isn't going anywhere.

I sit for a moment, just breathing. The last time I was here, I still had a future. Now, I'm not so sure. The medal on my chest weighs heavy. I step out of the truck, and I'm hit by a wall of humid, oppressive air. The sound of a bugle cuts through, sharp and lonely.

The VFW hall is a short walk from the square. A guard stands at attention, flags flapping lazily in the thick air. I pause at the door, take a deep breath and push inside.

The hall is a time capsule, stuck somewhere in the late seventies. Wood-paneled walls, mustard-yellow linoleum, a bar in the corner stocked with bottom-shelf liquor. The air conditioning struggles against the crowd, a mix of old-timers and young families. I recognize a few faces, but no one approaches me. Maybe they remember the kid who used to bus tables at Sal's Pizzeria or the young hotshot enlistee. More likely, they just know Emma.

I scan the room, and for a moment, I think she's not here. A foolish fear. Of course, she's here. Her father is a fixture at these things, and she—there she is.

Emma stands near the bar, talking to an older woman I dimly recognize as Mrs. Donahue, the high school librarian. She's wearing a simple, wollen blue dress that hugs her curves in all the right places. Her hair is longer than I remember, cascading over one shoulder in loose waves. She laughs at something the old woman says and the sound cuts through me like shrapnel. The smile doesn't reach her eyes like it used to. There's something guarded there now, something I put there the day I left.

Damn it. My chest tightens, and I grip my hands into fists. I shouldn't have come. I knew this would be hard, but seeing her—seeing her like this—is a different kind of pain. I turn to leave, but the door swings open, and I'm shoved back by a rush of bodies coming in from the square. Trapped, I make for the nearest exit, a side door that leads to a small patio. I'm almost there when I hear it.

"Cole?" Her voice is softer than I remember, or maybe it just seems that way because I can barely hear. I turn slowly, and there she is—closer now. Her eyes are the same clear green, like sea glass. Her lips part as if she's going to say something, then close. The silence stretches a tightrope over a canyon.

"Emma," I manage. My throat is dry, my words sandpaper. God, I've missed her so much.

Her arms are crossed, not in anger but in the way people do when trying to protect themselves. Her posture is straighter and more confident, but there's a fragility to it, like glass that's been tempered, made stronger by the flame but capable of shattering.

"I didn't know you were back," she says. It's not an accusation, but it's not neutral, either. She doesn't look away. Neither do I. But I see it. I see how she shifts and bites her lip, steeling herself. I see she's hurt. And I'm the bastard who did that.

"I'm not," I say. "Just here for the memorial." I fight the urge to get close, to explain the unexplainable. But that's the thing about pain; it doesn't make room for words. My feet are firmly planted on the spot. But my heart, my heart lunges forward, aching to reach her.

She nods, and her eyes flicker to the medal on my chest. "You earned it, you know."

"No," I say, too quickly, too sharply. "I didn't."

The hurt in her eyes is immediate and I realize she thinks I'm rejecting her attempt at kindness. I want to tell her everything—to unload the whole rotten truth—but there's no time. There's never enough time.

"Cole," she starts, but I cut her off.

"How's your dad?"

She hesitates, then sighs. "He's good. Stubborn as ever. He'll be glad to see you."

I doubt that. Frank was like a second father to me until I broke his little girl's heart. Until I broke her and then ran away like a coward.

"I should go say hi," I lie. "Take care, Emma."

I turn to leave, and this time, she doesn't stop me. How can I explain it? The mission, the boy, the crushing weight of survival. The fact that I don't even recognize myself anymore.

Not for a long time. I left because I couldn't face her. After all, I couldn't face anyone. Because I thought if I just disappeared, the pain would go away. I push through the side door and into the thick, soupy air of the patio. A small group of smokers huddle in one corner, talking in low, raspy voices. I loosen my tie and wipe the sweat from my forehead.

Why did I think I could do this? The memorial, the town, her. It's all too much, too soon. I stare at my reflection in the hall windows. My medal. Silver, with a star and a wreath. It's supposed to represent valor, but all I see is the face of the boy. He couldn't have been more than sixteen, and his eyes were so wide, so unbelieving. I had less than a second to decide.

The door swings open and I tense, hoping it is Emma. A tall man in a Marine dress uniform steps out, a cigarette already lit. He sees me and nods. I nod back. He doesn't say anything; he just takes a long drag and blows the smoke skyward. I envy him for his easy nonchalance. I used to be that guy.

The medal is now hot in my hand, like it's absorbed all the guilt and shame I've been carrying. I squeeze it tight, then let it clatter to the ground. The Marine looks over, but I'm already walking away.

I make it to the truck and sit, not moving, not thinking. Just staring at the empty passenger seat. A tap on the window startles me, and I flinch. I roll down the window.

"You forgot this, Sir," the Marine says, holding the medal. "Semper fi."

"Semper fi." I look down at the medal in my hand. It's crushed and bent out of shape from when I squeezed it too hard. I put it in my pocket and start the truck, and drive.

The streets of Haverhill blur together, a smear of memory and regret. I pass the high school, the old ball field, the diner where Emma and I had our first date. Everywhere I look, ghosts.

I pull onto the highway and flick on the A/C. It blows hot, useless air. My shirt is soaked through, my tie a noose. I loosen it, then take it off completely, tossing it onto the passenger seat.

The miles tick by, and I think about the boy again. About how he'll never grow up, never have a first kiss, never know the pain of losing someone he loves. I took all that from him, and for what? So my squad could live to fight another day, another battle, another war that none of us understand.

I thought the pain would dull over time, that the distance would help. But it's as sharp as ever, a knife in my side. The military cleared me, but I know the truth: I'm a murderer.

The exit for Haverhill comes up, and I take it. The truck winds through familiar streets, past the old textile mill, and along the river. I'm not ready to leave.

I find myself back in the town square. The crowd has dispersed, and the lawn is littered with paper flags and empty soda cans. I park and walk to the center of the square, where a granite monument stands tall and unyielding. Names are etched into its surface, a roll call of the dead.

I trace a finger along one of the names. Michael J. Thompson. We called him Mickey. He was the first of our crew to go, taken out by an IED in Kandahar. I remember his stupid grin and how he sang off-key in the Humvee. He has a plaque and a flag; his family gave him a proper funeral.

The boy won't have any of this. No monument, no memorial. Just a bullet point in a casualty report. I close my eyes and see his face again, and behind him, I see the faces of my squad. I made a choice. It was a shitty, impossible choice, but it was the only one I could live with.

I open my eyes and look at the names again. Each one is a story, a life cut short. I think about Emma, about the future we'd planned. About how I took that life and threw it away.

The medal is heavy in my pocket. I take it out, look at it, and kiss it. Then I place it at the base of the monument, among the flags and flowers.

It means something.

I walk back to the truck and feel lighter for the first time in two years.

FIRES AND FAULT LINES
EMMA

The café door jingles as it opens, and my heart drops to my toes. There he is—all six-foot-something of stubborn muscle and jaw-clenching arrogance, standing in the doorway like he owns the place. The sun pours in behind him, catching on the scruff along his jaw, his impossibly broad shoulders, and those damn piercing eyes that I swear see through people. I feel every muscle in my body go rigid. He's even more handsome than I remember, and that pisses me off.

I'm supposed to hate him. And I do—I do. But I'd be lying if I said my heart didn't skip a beat the second I saw him. I clench my fingers around the coffee pot in my hand, holding tight to the anger that's been keeping me upright these past two years.

Cole's eyes lock onto me the second he steps inside like he's tracking me. He strides across the café, ignoring the people who turn to look at him. He doesn't notice them. Doesn't notice anything, I think, except whatever mission he's got lodged in his thick skull.

He stops by the counter, hands braced on the edge as he leans in. "Emma."

I don't respond. I'm fixing a fresh cup of coffee for Mr. Henderson at the corner table, making sure the sugar's filled, refilling the cream. Anything to keep my hands busy, my heart steady.

"Emma," he says again, voice low and gruff.

I look up, forcing myself to look straight into his eyes. "Cole," I say his name with a sharpness that surprises even me. "What do you want? Aren't you gone yet? Veterans Day is over."

"I wanted to talk." His voice is smooth, the words laced with the quiet confidence that used to be so damn appealing. Now, it just grates.

"Talk?" I say, raising an eyebrow. "You didn't seem all that interested in talking when you vanished off the face of the earth." Cole's jaw tightens, but he doesn't flinch. Just stands there, looking like he's carved from stone, except for the way his eyes soften just a bit when they meet mine. "What is there to talk about, Cole?"

"About yesterday," he starts. "And everything else. I know I have no right to ask you to … but I just…I need you to hear me out."

I cross my arms over my chest, I want to be strong. I want to tell him to shove his explanations up you know where and go. "Yesterday was a surprise. I thought you were still in Alaska or wherever you went, finding yourself." But the memories are here, slamming into me like they haven't left. The way he used to be, the way he used to look at me like I was the only thing in the world that mattered.

"Please."

"Fine," I say, setting the coffee pot down a little harder than I mean to. "But make it quick. I've got customers."

His eyes flick over to where Mr. Henderson is now sitting with his newspaper, then over to the counter where another man, new in town, is sipping his coffee, scrolling through his phone and looking at me. A muscle jumps in his jaw as he spots him. I know that look, that possessive glint that says he doesn't like someone else in my space. I clench my teeth. After two years of silence, he's got no right to be jealous now.

"Well?" I press, folding my arms. "What do you want to say, Cole?"

He hesitates, running a hand over his face. For a split second, he looks tired. Tired in a way I haven't seen him before, and it throws me off balance. But I don't let my guard down. I can't afford to.

"There are things I can't explain, Emma," he finally says, his voice softer now. "Things I can't take back. But leaving— leaving you like that? It wasn't because I didn't care."

"Could've fooled me." I fire back, a little too harsh, but I can't help it. He left without a word, without a clue where he'd gone or if he'd ever come back. I waited, I worried, I put myself back together again, and here he is now like none of that ever happened. Like he can just walk in here and say a few words and make it better.

"Emma, please," he says, his voice quiet, almost pleading.

"What do you want me to say, Cole?" I demand, keeping my voice low so the customers can't hear. "That I understand? That I'm okay with being left in the dark while you took off to God knows where?"

He doesn't answer, but the look on his face tells me he's feeling the sting. Good.

"Just tell me one thing," I say finally clenching my fists. "Why? Why did you leave?"

Cole takes a breath, his shoulders rising and falling as he lets it out. "Because I thought you'd be better off without me," he admits, his voice barely above a whisper.

The words hit me harder than I expected, and for a moment, I'm not sure what to say. I look away, feeling the burn behind my eyes. "Well, you thought wrong," I manage, trying to keep my voice steady.

Just then, the new guy at the counter glances up and

catches my eye. He gives me a small smile like he's asking if I'm okay. Cole notices, and his jaw clenches so tight I half expect to hear it crack.

I raise an eyebrow, refusing to let him see how much his jealousy gets to me. "Jealous?" I ask, my arms crossed over my chest.

"Damn right I am." His voice is a low growl, and for a second, the old Cole—the one who used to hold me like I was his whole world—flares up in his eyes. "I don't like seeing another man look at you like that."

"Funny, since you didn't mind leaving me for two years." I snap back, hoping he can feel just an ounce of the anger that's been bubbling up inside me for so long. He tries to respond, but I cut him off. "You don't get to come back here and act like you care about who I talk to or what I do."

"Emma—" His voice is strained, struggling to control his anger. "I know I don't have the right to feel this way. But the thought of someone else..." He stops and looks away as if ashamed of the admission.

I shake my head, "You can't just walk back into my life like this, Cole." I feel I'm about to cry. "You don't get to come back and make me feel like this."

He looks at me, really looks at me, and I see the regret, the pain but also see the possessive fire. Still there.

Without warning, he steps closer, and before I know it, his lips are on mine, capturing my breath and every single protest. It's a kiss full of all the things we didn't say, a crash of everything pent-up between us. His hand slips to my waist, pulling me closer as if he's afraid to let me go.

And then, just as suddenly as it began, he pulls back, his eyes wild with something I can't quite name. He looks at me like he wants to say something, like he's on the edge of spilling every secret he's ever kept.

But he doesn't. He steps back, breathless and furious, "I'm

sorry, Emma," he says and then turns and walks out of the café, leaving me standing there, heart racing, wondering if he'll ever come back.

HELD BY A THREAD

COLE

I 'm outside Emma's house, my hand hovering over the door. My heartbeat is louder than the crickets, drowning out everything but the thought of her. I shouldn't be here. I keep telling myself that. Her words hang heavy in my head. But staying away? Not an option anymore. All I want is to claim her, to take her back as mine.

Finally, I knock, and when the door swings open, she's standing there in jeans and a soft gray sweater, her hair loose and messy like she's just tossed it up. We just look at each other for a second. I've got nothing to say that'll make up for the past two years, but I've got everything I need to say right here, all churning in my gut.

"Cole," she says, voice steady, a little guarded. She steps aside, nodding for me to come in. She's calm, unreadable even, but I can see the fire in her eyes. It's that fire that brought me back here, the one that's never let me forget her for a damn second.

The door closes with a soft click, and we're standing in her living room, surrounded by walls painted in warm, soft colors, the scent of her filling every corner. I drag my fingers through my hair, thinking of how to start this, what to say.

"I'm sorry, Emma," I say finally. "For all of it. For leaving, for everything I didn't say." I swallow hard, the words catching in my throat. "You deserve more than this, but I needed you to know... I never stopped loving you. Wanting you."

"You hurt me, Cole." Her arms are crossed over her luscious breasts, a tiny tremble in her fingers. "You just disappeared without a word. Like I didn't even matter."

"You mattered. You mattered more than anything," I say, her words a punch, direct and unforgiving, cutting right through me. "But I didn't think I was—am—enough for you any more."

She lets out a soft, frustrated laugh, shaking her head. "Enough? I didn't need perfect, Cole. I needed you. And you left."

I can feel her slipping through my fingers again, and the thought is unbearable. "Emma, I thought I was protecting you," I say, my voice barely above a whisper. "I thought if I stayed, I'd drag you down with me."

She moves closer and I can feel the heat of her anger, her hurt. "I didn't need protecting, Cole. I needed the man I loved to stay and fight for me. For us."

Fight for her. And just like that, the last of my restraint snaps. I reach for her and pull her against me. She doesn't resist; her hands rest against my chest, and that one small touch is enough.

"I can't be without you," I murmur, searching her eyes. I need her to feel every word I'm not saying out loud. "I can't do it anymore. Forgive me?"

Her breath catches, "Then don't leave again, Cole," she whispers. "Just don't leave me again."

That's it. That's all I need to hear.

My lips find hers, hungry. Her hands move up my neck, fingers tangling in my hair, and my grip tightens on her waist, pulling her closer. I'm sure she can feel my hardness. I kiss her harder, desperate, possessive, pouring everything I've kept locked inside into this one moment. She's mine. She always has been, even when I tried to convince myself she wasn't.

We stumble toward the couch, and she falls back, pulling me with her. My hands roam over her curves, every inch of her familiar. Every soft sound she makes sends a rush of need through me. Makes me harder. I don't think I'm going to last long. I kiss her like a man starved, like I've been craving this for two years—and hell, I have. Because being with Emma, feeling her pressed against me, fills the parts of me I thought were gone. I pull back just enough to look at her, my breath heavy, heart pounding.

"I'm broken baby. There's... things I've done." I rasp. "Things I can't take back."

She cups my face, her touch grounding me, softening me in a way that only she can. She knows I'm not whole, but somehow, she still wants me and sees something in me worth loving. I don't have an answer for that, not one that makes sense. So, instead, I show her. My lips find hers again, slower this time, deeper. I let myself sink into her, let myself feel every inch of her. And when she looks up at me, her eyes soft, I know there's no going back. I unbutton her jeans and pull them down. Her lacy panties come down too. She wiggles her hips and lift her neatly trimmed pussy, teasing me. I remove the rest of her clothes and free my hard cock.

"Open your legs baby," and I rub my leaking dick in her hot opening, around her clit.

"Oh...mmmh..."

"You like that baby?"

"Oh yes," she purrs. I can't wait any longer and my tip slides over her entrance.

"Ouch, baby, it hurts..." she moans. "I haven't...since you left..." That is so fucking hot.

"Relax baby, let me in," her nipples are hard and perky. I

need to be inside her now. "Hold on to the couch baby." I slide myself in a bit more and more.

"Cole," she whines.

"You were made to take me baby, remember?" I plunge in and her pussy is gripping me. I am trying to go as slow as I can, but all I want to do is slam in and make her mine. Again. And again, and again.

"Coooole ..." she gaps and he pussy loosens, releasing her tight grip. Her hips lift toward me, pushing my cock deeper.

"Oh my God, that's so good."

"That's right, baby," I slam forward. "You are mine...you... are...mine..." and with every word I fuck her harder. Two years of pent-up hunger for her. She pants, and the more she does, the harder I fuck her.

"Cole."

"SAY it again!"

"COOOLE!!!" She is screaming now. She screams as I pound her tight pussy over and over. I wait for her to go over the edge before I let myself come. Her hand rests against my chest, fingers splayed, and for a second, everything else fades. I lean down and press a kiss to her forehead, hoping she knows, hoping she understands everything I can't put into words.

STAY
COLE

The morning light slips through the blinds. I'm lying here beside her, wide awake. Her breathing is slow, steady—so peaceful that I barely let myself breathe, afraid to break the spell. She's curled into me, her body fitting against mine like this was always where she was meant to be. But the weight I thought I'd left outside her door last night comes crashing back. She deserves more. What if I lash out and hurt her? I slip out of bed carefully, trying not to wake her. Quietly, I slip out of bed and pull on my jeans. The floor is cold against my bare feet, a sharp contrast to the lingering heat of her body. I run a hand through my hair, take a deep breath, and head for the door.

I need air. I need to think. I need to figure out how the hell I'm going to do this.

The hallway is silent, the kind of silence that only exists in the early hours of the morning before the world has woken up. I make my way to the kitchen and pour myself a glass of water, staring out the window at the empty street. Memories of last night flicker in my mind: her touch, her kiss, the way she said my name.

I'm a fool. A damn fool. I should never have come back. The sound of footsteps pulls me from my thoughts. I turn to see Emma standing in the doorway, wrapped in a sheet. Her eyes are soft and vulnerable.

"Cole," she says. Just my name, but it's enough to break me. She doesn't move. "What are you doing?"

"I... I just needed a moment. I'm coming back."

"Don't lie to me." Her voice is steady. She knows me too well. "You're going to leave again."

I don't answer. I can't.

"Cole," she says, taking a step closer. "I can't do this if you're just going to disappear each time. I need to know what you want."

What I want. It's a simple question with an impossible answer. I want her. I want us. But more than that, I want her to be safe, to be happy.

"Emma," I start, but she cuts me off. "Emma, I don't think you understand—"

"I know who you are, Cole," she interrupts, her voice firmer. "I don't know exactly what you've done, what you've been through. But none of that changes how I feel."

"Emma—"

"You don't get to decide this for me, Cole." She steps closer, her voice softening. "You don't get to push me away because you think it'll keep me safe. Or until you've...fixed whatever it is… That's not your call to make."

I look at her, really look at her, and it's like I'm seeing her for the first time. She's stronger now. "I still love you," she says.

"I love you too baby," I say, and it's the truth. "I never stopped." I say, my voice rough.

She takes another step, and now she's close enough to touch.

I want to. God, I want to. But wanting has never been enough.

"I left to protect you," I say. "You know that."

"You didn't just leave me. You made the choice for me, like I'm some damsel in a fucking fairy tale. You don't get to decide what's best for me," she interrupts. "You're the only one who gets to decide who you are. But you don't get to decide for me." Her touch is gentle, but it undoes me. "You don't have to do this alone."

She lets the sheet drop from her shoulders. For a brief moment, she stands before me in all her naked, unguarded beauty. Then she turns and walks back to the bedroom.

I stand in the kitchen for a long time, staring at the empty doorway. The glass in my hand is warm now, the water undrinkable. I pour it out in the sink and run a hand over my face, exhausted.

Slowly, I make my way back to the bedroom. Emma is under the covers, her back to me. I strip off and slide into bed beside her, not touching, just close enough to feel the faint heat of her body. I'm done. Done fighting it. I know that I can't walk away from her again.

"I love you, Emma." I murmur, brushing a strand of hair from her face. "I thought I was doing the right thing by staying away. But God help me, I don't want to anymore."

She smiles softly and takes my hand, pressing it against her cheek. "Then don't. Stay."

For the first time in years, the weight in my chest feels lighter. It's bearable because she's with me, choosing me even when I can't understand why.

EPILOGUE

COLE

The town square is quiet this morning. The place that once felt so small and suffocating now feels like home. It's home. Emma's hand is warm in mine, her fingers laced through mine as we walk, her other hand resting on the gentle swell of her belly. Our daughter runs a few steps ahead, her laughter echoing as she chases a stray leaf that skitters across the cobblestones. The sight of her—of our life —grounds me, keeps me steady.

I look down at Emma, her face glowing with that unmistakable warmth I fell for. She looks up, catching me watching her, and a slow smile spreads across her face. "What?" she says, pretending she doesn't know exactly what's got me wrapped around her finger.

"Just thinking how I got lucky," I murmur, gently squeezing her hand.

Her eyes soften, and she leans into me, resting her head on my shoulder. "We both did," she whispers back, her voice filled with that calm certainty that's held me together these last five years.

Now, with her by my side, with our family growing,

everything just makes sense. Emma brought me back from the dark, and it's given me something solid to hold onto.

Our daughter runs back to us, her cheeks flushed from the cool morning air. She reaches up, arms outstretched, and I lift her onto my shoulders, her laughter rumbling right down into my chest. Emma rests a hand on my arm, and I feel her steady grip, grounding me as always.

We pass by the memorial in the center of the square, and I catch sight of the familiar names etched into the stone. The old weight, the guilt that used to follow me everywhere, hovers for just a second. But then Emma's hand slides into mine, her thumb brushing against my knuckles, reminding me that I don't carry that burden alone anymore.

"Thinking about them?" she asks softly, sensing the shift in my thoughts as she always does.

"Yeah," I admit. "I think about them a lot. About all of it."

She nods, her eyes never leaving mine. "You've honored them. You've more than honored them. And you don't have to keep punishing yourself."

It's something she's told me a hundred times over the years, and every time she says it, it sinks in just a little more. "Come on," she says, tugging me along. "Let's go get some breakfast before our little whirlwind here decides to run off on her own again."

I pull her close, pressing a kiss to her temple. "You know she gets that from you."

She laughs, that soft, melodic sound that always does me in. I wrap an arm around her, settling my hand protectively over her growing belly. "Thank you," I say quietly, the words catching in my throat.

"For what?"

"For seeing me when I couldn't see myself. For loving me enough to pull me out of that hell I couldn't get out of on my own."

She reaches up, cupping my face, and her smile is so full of love it's almost hard to take.

Our daughter tugs at my sleeve, breaking me from my thoughts. Her little hand reaches for Emma's. "Come on, Mama, I'm hungry!" she whines.

Emma laughs, taking her hand. "Alright, alright," she says. I trail behind, watching the two of them, my whole world wrapped up in them.

When we finally reach the café, Emma turns to me, her gaze tender, "Are you happy, Cole?" she asks, though she already knows the answer.

I let out a breath, pulling her close, our daughter wedged between us. "Better than happy. I'm whole."

THE HOT PRIEST

WELCOME TO ST. AGNES

The village of St. Agnes is as sleepy as ever, with its thatched-roof cottages and the single, crooked spire of the little Catholic church piercing the sky like a tired finger. I love the predictability of my hometown, where the most exciting news is Mrs. Henderson's cat stuck in a tree or the occasional bake sale.

"Sophia! Have you heard?" Clara comes running up, breathless and wide-eyed.

"Heard what?" I ask, curious but not overly so. Clara has a tendency to exaggerate.

"A new priest is coming to St. Agnes, Father Luca! Everyone is talking about him."

A new priest? I liked the old one. Father Thompson had been a fixture for as long as I can remember. Not that I go to church that much.

"Why on earth would they send a new one?" I ask though a small thrill runs through me. Change is afoot, and change is something I secretly crave, even if I would never admit it.

"I don't know," Clara says, shrugging. "But they say he's quite handsome."

Handsome? The notion is ridiculous. Priests are supposed

to be pious and humble, not dashing. I picture an older man with graying hair and kind eyes, someone scholarly and wise.

"He was a Marine, you know… before," Clara continues.

I think of war and women, an unholy past.

On the morning of his arrival, the village turns out in force. A small crowd gathers at the bus stop, peering down the winding road from the nearest market town. I stand on tiptoe, straining to see over the heads of my fellow villagers. I catch sight of Clara and wave; Clara blows a kiss and makes a swooning motion with her hand. I roll my eyes but can't suppress a grin.

The bus appears in a cloud of dust, wheezing to a stop with the creak of ancient brakes. The crowd grows silent, expectant. The door swings open, and a tall figure emerges, stretching as if uncoiling from a too-small box.

Oh my, oh my... This is no grizzled elder. He's tall, with salt and pepper hair cropped close to his head, and he's dressed in his priest's collar and black cassock, the fabric clinging to him in a way that defies the usual rules of modesty. I blink, struggling to tear my gaze away, but it's impossible. He's nothing like I imagined. He's... breathtaking.

"Dear God," someone whispers, though I can't tell who. I am too busy staring, my mind whirling with contradictory thoughts and emotions. Father Luca surveys the crowd with an air of detached curiosity. "Thank you for the warm welcome," he says, his voice a deep, velvety rumble. "I look forward to getting to know each of you."

My heart does a little flip.

The crowd begins to disperse, villagers muttering to each other . I linger, watching as Father Luca retrieves a battered suitcase from the bus driver. He glances in my direction, and our eyes meet for a brief, electrifying moment.

I turn away quickly, my cheeks burning, and start down

the lane toward my cottage. Halfway there, I stop and look back. Father Luca walks slowly, taking in the village as one might take in a new painting. He pauses outside the church, its weathered wooden door and stone façade standing in stark contrast to his sleek, black silhouette. His movements careful, measured. Like he's holding back something powerful.

I bite my lip and wonder what he is thinking. I wonder a lot of things. I shouldn't be looking at him like this. He's a priest for heaven's sake! A Catholic priest no less! But the more I watch him, the more I wonder—what if he wasn't?

The thought comes uninvited, and I press a hand to my mouth as if that could somehow push it away. But it doesn't.

Now only one thing is sure: St. Agnes is no longer the unchanging, predictable village I grew up in. And for the first time in my life, I'm not sure if that's a good thing or a bad thing.

CONSTRAINS

I become obsessed with the idea of breaking through his priestly exterior. Every encounter leaves me wanting more, my heart pounding at the thought of what could happen if he gave in to temptation. I never been to church this much in my life.

Today, I sit in the back of the small, dimly lit church, watching Father Luca prepare for Mass. His movements are deliberate, almost graceful, as he lights the candles on the altar and arranges the chalice and paten. There's a reverence in the way he goes about his tasks, a quiet devotion that makes my breath catch in my throat.

I shouldn't be here. It's a Tuesday morning, and I have a million other things I should be doing. But the pull to see him, to feel that electric charge when our eyes meet, is too strong to resist.

The handful of parishioners gathered for this weekday service rise to their feet as Father Luca takes his place at the lectern. I stand slowly, my eyes never leaving him. His voice is rich and warm as he recites the opening prayers.

Halfway through the service an older woman seated near the front collapses. There's a moment of stunned silence and, before people rush to her aid, Father Luca is at her side and helps her to a seated position. He speaks to her in low, soothing tones.

I should go down and see if she's all right, but I stay rooted to my spot, watching him. He's called to a higher purpose, I remind myself. This is who he is: a man of God, a servant of the people. Yet...

"I'm fine, I'm fine," Mrs Moore insists, "just a little light-headed." The congregation slowly returns to their seats. Father Luca insists she takes it easy and makes sure she has a ride home before resuming the service. He handles the whole situation with such calm authority that I feel a pang of something like pride. Or is it jealousy? I'm not sure anymore. Strong, manly, what a waste...

After Mass, I linger in the vestibule, pretending to read the announcements on the bulletin board. The other parishioners file out, offering Father Luca quick handshakes and words of thanks. I quickly peek in his direction and see him looking my way.

"Sophia," he says as he walks over to me. "It's good to see you. I didn't know you attended weekday Mass."

I shrug, trying to appear nonchalant. "It's a nice way to start the day."

He nods, and for a moment, we just stand there in an awkward pause.

"How are you? Really," he says, studying me.

It's a simple question, but it disarms me. How am I? Confused. Excited. Terrified. Desperate for something I can't have.

"I'm... good," I say, lying. "Busy with work, you know how it is."

He raises an eyebrow. "We all have our callings."

Callings. The word hangs in the air like incense, heavy and suffocating. I know what mine is, or at least what I want it to be.

"Father," I say as casually as I can manage. "Do you ever miss it? A regular life, I mean."

He raises an eyebrow, surprised by the question. "You mean the kind of life you have?" His tone is curious, not judgmental, and I wonder if he's interested.

"Yeah, I suppose." I shrug, pretending I don't care about the answer even though I do. "The freedom to make choices without... constraints."

He pauses, then leans in, lowering his voice. "My life was never quite... regular," he says first. "Freedom is relative, Sophia," he adds, the words a soft murmur, his eyes lingering on mine. "Sometimes, it's the constraints that keep us grounded." And then he steps back, a polite smile on his face, as though nothing has passed between us. Or did it?

"I should go," I say, though every part of me wants to stay. "I'll see you Sunday."

"See you at Mass," he says and I think I hear a note of reluctance in his voice. Or maybe it's hope. I can't tell anymore.

What am I doing? This can only end badly. For him, for me, for everyone.

But then I think of his eyes, how they look through me like he's trying to see my soul. I think of his hands, strong and steady, as he helped the old woman. Marine's hands. I think of his voice, the way it softens when he says my name.

I can't stop. I don't want to stop. My heart pounding at the thought of what could happen if he gave in to temptation.

What could happen?

I start the car and pull out of the parking lot, already counting the days until Sunday.

HONK HONK

I arrive home in a daze, the morning sun reflects on the cobblestone streets.

Inside my apartment, I kick off my shoes and collapse onto the sofa. The room is warm, almost stifling, but I make no move to open a window. I like the heat; it matches the slow burn that's taken up residence in my chest. I close my eyes and let my mind wander, drift back to the church. The moment replays in my mind like a scene from a forbidden romance novel. His eyes, the way they darkened, the silence that spoke volumes. I repeat our conversation in my head dissecting every word, every inflection.

"Sophia," the way he said my name with an intensity that made my breath catch. I imagine him saying it again, saying it the way a lover would, with need and urgency. I imagine him crossing the small, sacred space between us, his hands rough and desperate as they pull me into him.

The tension unbearable. I sit up, run my fingers through my hair, and then lie back down. I know I shouldn't be thinking like this. He's a priest, for God's sake. But the heart—and the body—wants what it wants, and right now every part of me is screaming for him.

I think about the confessionals, about slipping into one and baring my soul, telling him every sinful thought I've had since we met. Would he absolve me? Or would he be tempted to sin with me? The idea sends me into a shiver of fear and exhilaration. The questions swirl, mixing with the heady rush of what-ifs and maybes. I'm in too deep. I know that. This isn't some harmless crush; it's a full-blown obsession.

In my bedroom, I strip down to my underwear and flop onto the bed. The ceiling fan whirs lazily above me, but it does little to cool the flush that's spread across my skin. I reach for my phone on the nightstand, then think better of it. Who would I even talk to about this? Clara would have a fit; she already thinks I spend too much time at the church. And telling my mother is out of the question. This is something I have to deal with on my own.

I roll onto my side and hug a pillow to my chest. In my mind, I see him again, standing at the altar, his face a mask of conflict and desire. I imagine walking up to him, taking his hand, leading him away from the statues of saints and the flickering votive candles. We go to his office, where the walls are lined with books and the air smells of old paper and wood polish. He closes the door, and for a moment, we just stand there.

He breaks first, his lips crushing against mine with a hunger that's been building for weeks. I melt into him, my hands exploring the hard lines of his body beneath the soft fabric of his cassock. He tastes of wine and something sweeter, something I can't place but know I'll crave forever. We stumble against the desk, knocking over a stack of papers, and he lifts me and sets me down on the cluttered surface. His hands are everywhere—my hair, my waist, my thighs—and I arch into him, pulling him closer, needing more.

Honk, honk...

A car horn blares outside, yanking me back. I sit up, my skin tingling, my heart pounding as if I've just run a marathon. My nipples are hard and my panties are wet. This is dangerous. I'm playing with fire, and I know it. But the thought of damping these flames is more than I can bear.

Did he want me too? Or am I just projecting my own desires onto him? The uncertainty gnaws at me, but in a way, it also fuels the desire. The not knowing, the waiting, the tension—it's an addictive torture.

I get up, walk to the kitchen, open the fridge, and close it. I'm not hungry. I glance at the clock on the wall; it's only six. Gosh, six. Too early for bed, too late to start anything productive. I think about going for a walk but don't have the energy for it.

Back in the living room, I pick up a book, then put it down. Nothing can hold my attention. All I can think about is him, about us, about the line so precariously close to crossing. I know I should pull back, create some distance, but the thought of not seeing him, not feeling this electric charge, is unbearable.

I walk to the bathroom and turn on the shower. Steam fills the small space, and I let the hot water cascade over me, hoping it will wash away the longing, the confusion. It doesn't. If anything, it intensifies the ache. I play with myself. Slowly...intentionally... Ahh...my hand, his hand, Uhm... my fingers, his fingers... Haaaaah!!!!

Release.

I wrap myself in a towel, wipe a circle in the fogged-up mirror and stare at my reflection. I look different, older somehow. More womanly. I think about what Father Luca must see when he looks at me. A lost soul seeking guidance? A temptress? I don't even know who I am anymore.

I dry off and slip into my nightgown, then pad back to the

living room. The sun has dipped below the horizon. I like this time of day, the in-betweenness of it. It's a time for possibilities, for dreams that haven't yet been crushed by the stark light of morning.

My phone buzzes, and I jump. For a moment, I let it sit, afraid to see who it might be. Then I reach for it, my hands trembling slightly.

It's a text from Clara.

"Wine night?"

I hesitate. I could use the distraction, the company. But I also know that Clara will want to talk, and I'm not sure I can keep this all inside if she starts asking questions.

"Can't tonight. Sorry,"

I type, then add,

"Rain check?"

I hit send and feel an immediate wave of relief, then guilt. I do want to see her, just not tonight. Tonight, I need to sit with this, to figure out what the hell I'm going to do.

I pour myself a glass of wine and take it to the sofa, curling up with a blanket. Just one glass I tell myself knowing full well I'll finish the bottle. The first sip goes straight to my head, and I let out a small, contented sigh.

My thoughts drift back to Father Luca, as they always do now.

Is it love? Lust? Some twisted form of spiritual longing? I don't know, and the not knowing is driving me mad.

I finish the glass and pour another, the bottle now empty. The wine has loosened me, making my thoughts less jagged and more fluid. I let them flow where they will, unrestrained.

What if he did succumb? The question lingers, and I let it. I picture him at my door, his face a storm of emotions. He wouldn't need to say anything; I would just know. I invite him in, and for a moment, we stand in the hallway, the air thick with anticipation. Then he takes me in his arms, and it's exactly as I imagined—fierce, urgent, unstoppable.

We make our way to the bedroom, shedding clothes and inhibitions. His hands are skilled, his mouth worshipful. Every touch is a confession, every kiss an absolution. We sin and save each other in the same breath, the same motion. It's everything I've dreamed and more, so much more that it overwhelms me and consumes me.

I wake to find him dressing, his movements slow and reluctant. He looks at me, and in his eyes, I see a man torn in two. "I have to go," he says, but I hear the unspoken "I don't want to" beneath it.

"Will I see you again?" I ask, though I already know the answer.

He walks to the door, pauses, then turns back. "Sophia," he says, and how he lingers on my name makes my heart break and soar all at once. Then he's gone, and I'm left with the ghost of his touch and the hollow ache of something beautiful and fleeting. God, I sound like a trashy romance novelist.

The empty wine glass slips from my hand and clatters onto the coffee table, startling me from my reverie. I stretch and yawn, the alcohol making me drowsy. For a moment, I consider going to bed, but then I remember the bottle of Limoncello in the freezer. It's my grandmother's recipe, potent and syrupy-sweet.

I retrieve the bottle and pour a small amount into a glass, the cold liquid glowing neon in the dim light. I take a tentative sip, and it burns in the most delightful way. The Limoncello is working its magic, blurring the edges of my thoughts even more and making everything seem less dire. I can almost convince myself that this is just a phase, that I'll wake up one morning and the attraction will have evaporated, leaving me free and unburdened.

Almost.

The glass is empty, and I contemplate refilling it, but decide against it. I'm already tipsy, and any more would tip me into drunk. I like this in-between state, where I'm floaty and light but still have a tenuous grasp on reality.

I think about him again, about his dedication, his vows. Could I really ask him to give all that up? The answer is obvious, but it doesn't stop me from wanting him to. It doesn't stop me from wanting him, period. Because as torturous as it is, this longing makes me feel alive. And that's something I haven't felt in a very long time.

I get up and walk to the bedroom. The night outside is still and quiet. I slip under the covers and close my eyes, hoping sleep will take me quickly. I drift off, not into sleep, but into a hazy half-dream where his hands are on me, his lips speaking words of love and sin. The fan above me casts slow, hypnotic shadows, and I surrender to them, to him, to the delicious agony of wanting.

NOT HERE

I wake up in a stupor, soaking wet, my head tumping. I can't do this any more. I can't until Sunday. I have to know. Today.

I wait until the evening. The church is empty. Shadows stretch across the benches, pooling in the corners as I step through the heavy wooden doors. My heart is pounding so loud it almost drowns out the quiet echo of my footsteps. I know he'll be here. He's always here late, preparing, praying, or maybe just hiding from the world.

Father Luca stands at the altar, his back to me, moving candles around, setting things in perfect order for tomorrow's service. There's something strangely vulnerable about him now—just him, alone in the quiet, dim light. But even with his back turned, the pull is undeniable. Like he knows I'm here, feels it in the marrow of his bones.

He turns, and his eyes find me instantly, a flicker of surprise, and then something else—a flicker of heat. "Sophia," he says, his voice low and rough, like gravel underfoot. "It's late. What are you doing here? Is everything all right?"

I swallow, my heart racing as I move a step closer, feeling

the intensity in his gaze settle like a weight on my skin. "I... I wanted to see you," I say, my voice barely a whisper.

He watches me in silence, his eyes dark, assessing, and so full of things I can't quite read. The air thickens between us, every unspoken word, every lingering look from the past few weeks pressing down on us, binding us closer.

I let out a shaky breath, taking another step. "I know I shouldn't... but I can't help myself."

His expression shifts, something raw flickering in his eyes before he looks away, jaw tight. "Sophia, you know this... it's not right."

He doesn't move, doesn't step back. And neither do I.

"But I think you want this too," I murmur, barely daring to breathe. "Don't you?"

For a second, he says nothing, just stares at me, his eyes burning, before he slowly nods. "I do. God help me, I do."

The confession hangs between us, heavy and undeniable. I close the last bit of space between us, reaching out to brush my fingers over his hand, my heart racing so fast I can hardly keep my thoughts straight. His skin is warm, almost searing, and a shiver runs through me at the simple touch.

He doesn't pull away, doesn't even flinch. He looks like a man barely holding on, barely containing something wild and dangerous beneath that calm exterior.

"Sophia..." he whispers, his voice hoarse, full of an unspoken longing. "You don't know what you're doing to me."

I lean in closer, my heart pounding against my ribs. "Then show me." For a heartbeat, he stands there, staring at me, like he's fighting some internal battle, his brows drawn, his jaw tense. And then, something snaps. His hand moves up to my wrist, holding it with a grip that's firm, possessive, yet achingly gentle.

A thrill rushes through me at his words, knowing I have this effect on him, knowing he feels the same relentless pull that's been consuming me. "Don't stop," I whisper, running my fingers along the line of his jaw, feeling the tension there, the strength and softness in one touch.

"Not here…" he says before he turns away. "God, forgive me," he whispers genuflecting in front of the altar.

"Come."

GOD FORGIVE ME

I follow him into his office. He closes the door behind us and turns the key. The controlled, holy priest is gone, replaced by a man consumed by desire for me. His alpha nature takes over. Father Luca pulls me into a corner, his lips claiming mine with a raw, unrestrained passion.This is no tentative first kiss; it's an explosion, a release of all the longing and restraint that have been building for weeks.He wants me, needs me, and gives in to the passion that's been building between us for weeks, sharing a night of intense, forbidden pleasure.

This is wrong.

This is so, so wrong.

But God forgive me, it feels so right.

His hands are everywhere, rough and insistent, as if he's afraid I'll disappear if he doesn't hold me tight enough. I run my fingers through his thick hair, pulling him closer, closer. His stubble scrapes against my skin, a delicious contrast to the heat of his mouth.

He breaks away, breathing hard.

Oh God, if he stops now, I'll shatter. I need this. I need him. The guilt can come later.

"Sophia," he whispers my name and the sound is molten, loaded with a desire that makes my knees weak,"I can't fight this anymore. I can't fight the way I feel." His hands find my waist, gripping me with a force that pulls me against his body. I can feel the hard lines of him through his clerical vestments, the heat radiating from his skin. I can feel he is hard. Every touch, every movement is charged with the full force of his alpha possessiveness. He kisses me like a man starved, like he's been dying for this and can't get enough. I'm drowning in him, in the taste of his lips and the rough scrape of his stubble. A small voice in the back of my mind tells me this is madness, that we're crossing a line we can never uncross, but it's drowned out by the rush of blood in my ears and the thudding of my heart.

We are a tangle of limbs and clothing, stripping away the barriers between us with a frantic urgency. His cassock lies in a heap on the floor, a black puddle of discarded virtue. I take in the sight of him, lean and muscular. His scars, the tattoos. His incredibly massive erected penis. I don't think I can take him.

He pulls me up and I wrap my legs around his waist. The wall is cold against my back. He kisses my neck, my collarbone, his breath hot and ragged. I arch into him, desperate for more.

"Luca," I gasp, and the sound of his name seems to push him over the edge.

"Say it again," he orders me.

"Lu..c..a.."He holds me up with one hand while the other caresses my opening. "Uhm…Ahh…"

"You like that?" He says and pushes one finger inside.

"Oh yes…" Two fingers. In and and out. In and out.

"Luca … I… more…" And he obliges taking me with a force that borders on violence; each thrust a confession, a penance, an absolution. I bite down on his shoulder to keep from crying out, the pain and pleasure mingling in a dizzying, intoxicating swirl.

We collapse onto the narrow cot in the corner of his office. He strokes my hair, my cheek, his touch suddenly tender. I close my eyes and let myself drift, not wanting to face the reality of what we've done.

"Forgive me," he whispers, and I don't know if he's asking for my forgiveness or God's. Maybe both.

I open my eyes and look at him, this man who has torn my soul in two. One-half lies in ruins, crushed by the weight of our transgression. The other half burns with a fierce, unholy joy.

"Luca," I say, and my voice is soft, fragile. "What happens now?"

He doesn't answer, and I know that he can't. That we can't. This was a moment stolen from time, a reckless plunge into the abyss. We can't live here.

But for now, we linger.

For now, we breathe.

EPILOGUE

The church bells ring out, filling the air with a warmth that pulses straight into my chest. I open my eyes slowly, letting the sound settle into my bones. Today's the day. The day where everything falls into place.

I take a breath, stilling the butterflies flapping around in my stomach since sunrise. The room is filled with soft morning light, spilling across the lace of my dress laid carefully on the bed. I run my fingers over it, feeling the fabric, grounding myself in this moment. It's surreal, almost like I'm in a dream, but this time I know it's real.

The reflection in the mirror smiles back at me, cheeks flushed, eyes bright, lips pulled into a nervous grin. This is it. The end of one chapter and the start of something new, something deeply real. A knock at the door brings me back to the present.

"It's time, Soph," my mom's voice calls softly from the other side.

I take one last look at myself in the mirror, smoothing down the dress as I nod to the woman I see. Today isn't about fantasy or fleeting desire. It's about love that feels like home. It's about forever.

The short walk to the church feels like a hundred years and a single breath all at once. My family is here, my friends, all waiting, all here to witness me stepping into the next part of my life.

As I enter the church, the sound of quiet murmurs and shuffling feet fades away, replaced by the soft rustle of my dress and the steady beat of my heart. The aisle stretches out before me, flanked by rows of familiar faces, all smiling and glowing with warmth. And then, I see him—standing at the altar, his eyes kind and his face calm as he waits for me to walk toward him.

As I step forward, my heart skips a beat, passing rows of loved ones and friends. With each step, I let go of the dreams that once seemed so alluring, so forbidden. I almost laugh, but it's a quiet laugh tucked under my breath as I walk down the aisle, heart racing, a grin tugging at my lips. It's funny how something that felt so real was nothing more than a figment of my imagination. The fantasy of Father Luca was never about him, not really. It was about me, discovering what I wanted, my inner deeper desires, even if it was tangled up in a little chaos. Sometimes, we need that wildness to find what we truly crave. And now I know.

Paul turns as I reach the altar his gaze finding mine. His eyes are filled with warmth, love, and the kind of forever I want. His smile spreads slowly, lighting up his face, and my heart beats a little faster, a little more sure. This man—*my man*—is my future. And I am ready for it, all of it.

I step forward, and he takes my hand, his fingers warm and steady against mine. For a moment, everything around us falls away. It's just us, here, standing on the edge of everything we're about to build together.

"You look amazing," Paul whispers, his voice soft but certain, and it sends a thrill through me.

I smile up at him, feeling the weight of the past slip away as I look at him. "So do you," I reply, and it's true. He looks like he belongs beside me like he's been waiting just for me, just for this.

Father Luca clears his throat, bringing us both back to the present. His eyes hold a knowing gleam, almost a spark of mischief, as though he's aware of the dreams that swirled through my mind leading up to today. I blush, casting my eyes down briefly, before lifting them again, stronger this time.

As the ceremony begins, I let myself sink into the words and promises, each echoing with a certainty that settles into my very bones. This is real. This is lasting. This is exactly what I was meant to find.

Now, I am exactly where I am meant to be, with exactly the person who's meant to be standing beside me.

And as I look into his eyes I realize that love doesn't have to be wild or forbidden to feel intense. Sometimes, the strongest love is the one that grounds you, that holds you steady when the world seems to spin around you.

The ceremony draws to a close, and we share a smile—one that feels like coming home. I can feel the warmth of his hand and the weight of the ring he just placed on my finger.

As we turn to face our family and friends, to step into the world together, I take one last look back at Father Luca, at the man who, for a short time, was the keeper of my wildest dreams. He nods, a faint smile on his lips, and I nod back, thanking him in my own quiet way.

Then, my husband squeezes my hand, and I turn to him, ready for whatever comes next. I know now that fantasy has its place, but reality—*this* reality—is what I want, what I need.

THE BAD SANTA

PROLOGUE
LOGAN

The snow falls in fat, lazy flakes, coating the town in a postcard-perfect blanket of white. I take it all in from the window of O'Malley's, nursing a coffee long since gone cold.

I fucking hate Christmas. The thing about Christmas is that it's all a lie. The happiness, the togetherness, the fucking goodwill toward men. It's a con job, a Hallmark card illusion that dissolves the second the tinsel comes down. I've seen too much, lived too much to buy into it anymore.

"Logan, you want a warm-up?" Maureen O'Malley, the owner and namesake of the town's only bar, holds a pot of coffee in one hand and cocks her hip to the side. She's a handsome woman in her fifties, with the bone structure that could cut glass and a shock of red hair starting to go white at the temples.

"I'm good," I say, though my voice comes out more growl than words. She shrugs and walks back to the bar, where a group of guys I went to high school with are working their way through a pitcher of beer. It's not even noon yet, but they're all home for the holidays, taking time off from whatever dead-end jobs they landed after college. The sound of their laughter sets my teeth on edge.

I should be one of them. That's the thing that pisses me off the most. I had it all: the girl, the future. Life has a way of disappointing you, of taking what you want most and crushing it in its fists.

A blast of cold air hits me as the door to O'Malley's swings open. A young couple walks in, the guy shaking snow from his hair, the girl holding a box of something wrapped in gaudy, glittering paper. They kiss, and it makes me feel sick.

I stand up, put on my coat, and walk to the bar. Maureen gives me a look that says she knows what I'm about to ask and doesn't approve. I don't care.

"Put it on my tab," I say. She slides a flask across the bar, and I pocket it without a word. The guys from high school stop their reminiscing long enough to nod in my direction. I nod back, then make for the door.

MISS CHRISTMAS

LOGAN

The town square's got the same saccharine every year—the fairy lights strung up like we're living in a snow globe, the wreaths on every door, and the damn candy cane poles lining Main Street. The only thing missing is a soundtrack of jingling bells and some overly cheerful elf handing out hot chocolate. People seem to love it—cheer plastered on their faces, kids buzzing around the vendors set up for the big holiday festival. All I see is a bunch of adults who've lost their damn minds over a few lights and a snowflake or two. And, of course, I'm right in the middle of it, like some unholy sacrifice to the gods of small-town cheer.

I've dodged this circus for years. If I could avoid stepping foot in town altogether, I would. But this is the one place with the hardware store that carries the parts I need to fix up the cabin.

"Mr Carter?Hey!" A woman's voice cuts through the holiday chaos, a voice that's somehow loud and soft at the same time. I don't recognize it, but the way it carries, honey-sweet and certain, pulls me up short. I turn, figuring it's some town newbie who hasn't heard I'm not big on chitchat. My tolerance for cheerful people, especially the ones that actually seem to enjoy this season, is low on a good day. On festival time? It's below zero.

She's...well, she's a lot. Bright blonde curls sticking out from under a green knit beanie, cheeks rosy from the cold, and a red scarf that's probably the size of a small country wrapped around her neck, practically glowing in the snow.

Great. I've been caught by Christmas incarnate.

Her smile's so wide it practically knocks the breath out of me. And those curves...well, let's just say they're noticeable, enough to make a guy start wondering. She doesn't waste a second, blinking up at me with these bright green eyes. "You're Logan Carter, right?" she asks, her voice lilting like a song. Her smile is way too friendly for a stranger's, and her eyes spark with mischief. "Just the man I was hoping to find. I'm Clara. The festival coordinator."

My stomach sinks a little. I know where this is going. But I'm not about to make this easy on her.

"Of course you are" I say folding my arms and leaning back on one foot. There's something about her that already has me on edge. Maybe it's the holiday overload or the way she's standing there like she's made of glitter and holiday spirit.

"What? You need someone to haul trees, deck halls..."

Her eyes brighten, and it's like a trap snapping shut.

"As a matter of fact..." She lifts an eyebrow. "You heard about Bob, Mr. Walsh, right? How he broke his leg?"

I grit my teeth, my gaze narrowing on her. "Unfortunate."

"Yes, very," she says, nodding like a bobblehead. "Which leaves us in a bit of a bind for the festival. You see, without a Santa—"

"No."

"Mr Carter, please. You're the only one who can pull it off on such short notice. The kids are counting on us."

"Well, I've got things to do," I say, still trying to wrap my head around the fact that people like her exist.

She lets out a laugh—soft, light, and way too tempting. "What kind of things? It's for the children…"

The nerve of this woman. But the way she's looking at me, with that expectant spark in her eye, that maddening smile and that glorious ass…

"Lady, you've got the wrong guy," I can't help the scoff that escapes. "I don't do Christmas, and I definitely don't do Santa."

She shrugs, her face still bright. "It could be fun. Besides, you'd be perfect, especially with that scowl. The kids will take you seriously." She gives me a sly little smile like she knows she's getting to me, even if it's just a little. I've just been hit by a freight train of Christmas spirit and curves I have no business thinking about.

I shake my head, feeling something strange stir in my chest. "Nope," I say side-stepping her.

Just when I think I've shaken her off, she calls over my shoulder, "Logan, wait!" And the way she says my name? Feels like a promise. Fuck.

THE GRINCH

CLARA

I straighten my scarf against the chill as I follow him into the hardware store, all six-foot-five something of raw irritation and the kind of broad shoulders that shouldn't be allowed in civilian life. But the thought of facing the festival without a Santa? Unthinkable. I've poured way too much time and energy into this holiday event, and I'm not about to let it flop.

The only issue is who I'm left with.

Logan Carter. The resident grump, infamous town Grinch, and precisely the last person I'd ever imagine coaxing into a Santa suit.

"Logan, wait…"

His eyes meet mine, a steely, intense gray that makes my stomach do a little flip before I can control it.

His expression darkens, if that's even possible. "What, you didn't get the message? I'm allergic to Christmas cheer."

I let out a laugh, mostly because it's either that or run away. "Yeah, well, I'm not trying to fill your house with poinsettias and carolers. But I do need your help." I take a step closer, lifting my chin. "As in, the entire town needs your help."

Logan's face goes blank for a second. Then, with a disbelieving shake of his head, he steps back, practically slamming the door as he mutters, "Absolutely not."

"Logan—wait!" I wedge my foot in the door before it shuts completely, ignoring the sting. I take a step closer so we're almost nose to chest. He's ridiculously tall, and I have to crane my neck to look up at him. "I wouldn't be here if I had any other option. It's less than a week to the Christmas's Eve Santa's grotto."

I lean my shoulder against the door, giving him my best pleading look. "Come on, it's just a couple of hours of sitting in a chair, handing out candy canes. You don't even have to smile. Just grunt a little—it'll probably seem authentic."

The corner of his mouth twitches, but he covers it quickly. "No."

"You're really saying no to helping out a town full of kids who are excited to see Santa?"

"Yes. Yes, I am. I hate Christmas. I hate the fake cheer, the forced traditions, and most of all, I hate the idea of being pushed into something so utterly ridiculous."

I take a step back, but not out of fear, the tension between us too much for my body to handle. "Fine," I say, throwing up my hands. "I get it. You hate everything. But just so you know, this isn't about you. It's about the town. It's about the kids. It's about tradition." I cross my arms, mirroring his stance. "If you just do this, I swear I'll make it up to you somehow. Think of the goodwill, the holiday spirit…"

His eyes roll so hard I'm half-surprised he doesn't get dizzy. "Holiday spirit? Don't tell me you believe in all that snowflake-and-sugar-cookie nonsense."

"Duh? Some of us enjoy being happy during the holidays," I reply.

A strange look crosses his face like he doesn't quite know what to do with that, and for a beat, we just stand there, staring each other down.

"Come on..." I say softly, my voice gentler. "It's a small thing. For a good cause. And—" I hesitate, adding quietly, "it would really help me out."

He lets out a long-suffering sigh, raking a hand through his dark hair, and for a second, I think I might've broken through. But he just shakes his head again, crossing his arms even tighter. "All I need is for you to sit in a chair. No other festival stuff. I promise. That can't be so hard, even for you, right?"

Logan stares at me, a glint of irritation in his eyes, and then, to my surprise, he mutters something under his breath and steps back from the door. "Fine. But you owe me," he says, his voice a low rumble.

I can't help the grin that breaks out on my face. "Deal! Now, about the Santa suit..."

BAD SANTA

CLARA

I wait in the lobby of Mrs. Thompson's Costume Emporium. Logan is late, and I start to wonder if he's bailed on me. I shouldn't be surprised; this is Logan we're talking about. But just as I'm about to give up and leave, the door jingles, and he walks in, a dusting of snow on his hair and shoulders.

"Sorry," he mutters. "Got held up."

I don't ask by what. Instead, I just smile and lead him to the back of the store, where Mrs. Thompson is waiting with the Santa suit. She's a tiny woman, well into her eighties, with hands that shake like leaves in a breeze. But her eyes are sharp, and she gives Logan an appraising look as we walk up.

"Logan, this is Mrs. Thompson."

"This is the new Santa?" she asks, skeptical.

"Temporary Santa," Logan corrects.

"He'll do," I say, ignoring them both. "Try it on."

He glares at me, one eyebrow raised. "You're really gonna stand there and watch?"

"OK, then .. There's a dressing room in the back," I say, pointing, "but I need to make sure you're...authentic-looking." Logan quickly disappears into the dressing room. I turn to Mrs. Thompson, and she raises an eyebrow at me; I know what she's thinking. The whole town knows about Logan and his Christmas boycott. They also know that I take the festival very, very seriously. Asking Logan to play Santa is like asking a vegan to carve the Thanksgiving turkey.

"It'll be fine," I tell her, and maybe myself. "He's doing it for the kids." She shrugs and totters off, leaving me alone in the fitting area. I start to hum "Jingle Bells," then stop myself. Logan would probably burst out of the dressing room and strangle me with tinsel if he heard.

"Hey, Miss Christmas," he calls, and I snap to attention. "I need help with the belt."

I hesitate for a moment, then walk to the dressing room door. It's cracked open just enough for me to see his face, and he steps back to let me in. The space is tiny, and with Logan in the Santa suit, it feels like a dollhouse. He towers over me, a red and white mountain of faux fur and padding. And a delicious salt and pepper beard, full lips...

I reach for the belt, and our hands brush. His skin is warm, almost hot, and I pull back instinctively. "Sorry," I say, then take the belt from him and start to wrap it around his waist. He has to suck in his gut—well, the stuffed gut of the suit.

"This thing is ridiculous," he grumbles.

He looks...well, he looks like an irritable, rough-around-the-edges Santa with biceps that might just be illegal for the part. I can't help the smile spreading across my face, but I keep it in check, or at least try to.

"See? You look the part already," I say, giving him a nod of approval.

Logan just shakes his head, shooting me a look that's equal parts smirk and scowl. "If you laugh, I swear..."

"Wouldn't dream of it," I reply, biting back a grin.

He looks down at me, and I realize how close we are. I can smell the faint scent of pine on him and it mixes oddly well with the synthetic Christmas aroma of the suit. My heart does a stupid little flutter, and I curse it for being so easily swayed by a man in costume.

"So," he says, and his voice has a different tone to it. Softer, maybe. "How did you get roped into running the festival, anyway? I thought it was Mrs. Kelley's thing."

I take a step back or try to. The wall of coats behind me stops my retreat. "Mrs. Kelley moved to Florida. Someone had to take over."

He nods as if this explains everything. "It's a lot of work. Do you even enjoy it?"

I blink, surprised by the question. "Of course I do. Christmas is—"

"The most wonderful time of the year," he finishes for me, but there's no mocking in his voice. It's flat, like he's reciting a fact from a textbook.

"Yes," I say more quietly. "It is."

We stand there in silence, and I start to feel uncomfortable in a way that's completely new. It's not his grumpiness that's getting to me; it's the lack of it. Without his usual surliness as a buffer, I'm left exposed to… I don't even know what. Whatever this is.

"I think the kids will buy it," he says, breaking the silence. He adjusts the hat on his head, and I have to admit, he looks the part. If I didn't know better, I'd think he was actually starting to get into it.

"They will," I say. "Better still. Try this on… for authenticity," I tease shoving a false white beard in his hand.

"Not a chance," he growls, tossing it right back at me.

I catch it with a smirk. "Fine, fine. Bad Santa's gotta keep his image intact, after all."

"Damn straight," he replies.

"Thank you, Logan. Really."

He opens the dressing room door, and cold air rushes in,

cutting through the warmth that had started to build. "Don't thank me yet," he says. "I haven't done anything."

I watch him walk out and something tightens in my chest. Maybe it's fear that he'll back out or hope that he'll come around. Or maybe it's just the sight of him, looking so out of place and yet so right.

PASSING BY

LOGAN

I shove my hands into my pockets and watch Clara bustle around the square, stringing lights between the big pine trees that surround the town's gazebo. She's everywhere—darting from one corner to the next, calling out orders like she's a general preparing troops for battle.

But despite myself, I can't stop looking at her.

Sunlight's catching her hair, bouncing off those curls in all directions, and every time she pauses to make sure a wreath is hanging just right or the tinsel's perfectly draped, I notice her biting her lip in concentration. It's distracting—more than it should be. And that laugh of hers? It grates on me in the worst kind of way, sticking in my head like a song you can't shake. I should be annoyed, but hell, she's right there, sparkling like a damn Christmas light herself.

"Oh, Logan, there you are!" she calls out, her face lighting up when she spots me lurking behind one of the trees. She's beaming. "Did you come to help?" she asks like she's already planning a thousand ways to pull me into this nonsense.

"Nope," I say flatly. "Just passing by."

She shakes her head, a small smile on her lips. "Right. And Santa doesn't like cookies." She skips over, holding up a tangled string of lights. "But if you're 'just passing by,' maybe you can pass me this up to the next branch."

"Really? You don't have anyone else to torture with this?" I raise an eyebrow, my voice dripping with sarcasm, but damn if I don't find myself reaching for the lights anyway.

She shrugs, her eyes twinkling. "Oh, you're the perfect man for the job, Bad Santa. Besides, I need someone tall."

I snort. "There's plenty of tall people in this town, you know. Probably ones who don't mind Christmas so much."

She just smirks, nudging the ladder my way, her hand brushing against mine. For a second, I almost forget to breathe. "Well, but you are here, so there you go," she says, giving me a wink.

This woman's playing with fire, and she knows it. I glare at her, but it's hard to keep the scowl when she's grinning up at me like that. I grunt and climb the ladder, reaching up to hook the lights over the branches.

"There. Happy now?"

"Thrilled." She clasps her hands together, looking genuinely delighted, and somehow that only irritates me more. "Maybe you're getting into the spirit after all."

"Don't count on it," I mutter, but she just laughs, and it's like she sees right through me. There's a tug of something in my chest that I can't quite shake and it only gets worse as the day goes on.

I can't stay away. I try to ignore her, to pretend I don't see the way her face lights up every time a kid waves to her or the way she scrunches her nose when she's deep in thought, but it's impossible. She's right there, getting under my skin.

"Clara, how about like this?" Charlie, the new guy in town, is calling for her attention. He is helping her hang garlands around the pavilion. He's smiling, laughing with her, and the way he's looking at her... makes my blood simmer. I know what he wants. What I want... She's laughing, probably saying something sweet. His eyes are practically glued to her curves.

I grit my teeth, fists clenching. "Clara," I call, my voice a low warning.

She turns, brows raised. "Yes, Logan?" Her smile slips into something more curious as I step closer, deliberately positioning myself between her and Charlie.

"Need help with anything else?" My tone is sharper than I intend, but I can't shake the irritation swirling in my chest.

She eyes me, her lips quirking into a knowing grin. "Well, well, maybe Bad Santa *is* feeling helpful." She places a hand on her hip, looking at me with a mischievous glint. "I thought you were 'just passing by.'"

"Changed my mind," I mutter, not breaking eye contact.

Charlie clears his throat, glancing between us. "Hey, Clara, I'll go grab those extra bulbs for you." He hurries off, clearly reading the tension. Good. Get the fuck out of here. The last thing I need is another guy sniffing around her, Christmas help or no.

She watches Charlie go, then raises an eyebrow at me. "Didn't know you were the protective type, Logan."

"I'm not," I grumble, stepping back. But the way she's looking at me, half-smiling like she's just cracked some secret code, makes me want to pull her close and prove just how wrong she is.

The afternoon winds down, and most of the others head home, leaving us to finish up some last-minute decorations. The sky's starting to darken, and the temperature's dropped, making everything feel quieter, more intimate.

"Hand me that last bit of mistletoe," she says, gesturing to a small branch of green with berries hanging from the end.

I grab it, handing it to her, but instead of taking it, she reaches up to hook it onto the branch between us, her fingers brushing mine as she does. My hand tingles from the touch, and it takes me a second too long to let go.

When she's done, she steps back, looking up at the mistletoe with a smile. "Perfect. Now, everyone who walks by will get a little dose of Christmas magic."

I'm not thinking about mistletoe or magic. I'm thinking about how close she is, how her breath turns into a soft cloud in the air, how her cheeks are flushed from the cold and maybe—just maybe—from me standing here, practically toe to toe with her.

Her eyes meet mine, wide and curious, and suddenly, I can't look away. I should. I know I should. But the warmth radiating off her, the way her scent fills the space between us —it's too much. Too tempting.

She clears her throat, breaking the silence. "Well, uh, I guess that's everything, right?"

"Right," I mutter, but I'm not moving. And neither is she. We're both standing here like two fools in the cold, and all I can think about is how much I want to pull her close and feel her in my arms, to taste that stubborn little smile of hers.

"Logan..." she whispers, her voice soft and a little shaky, like she's feeling the same thing I am.

I open my mouth, but nothing comes out. Words don't seem enough, not for this. All I know is that this woman, this Christmas-obsessed, infuriating, captivating woman, has somehow managed to crack the walls I've kept around my heart for years.

"Guess you're not such a Grinch after all," she says with a small smile, and for the first time, I don't have a comeback. I just watch her, wondering how the hell this woman managed to slip under my skin.

I want her. God, I want her.

But wanting and having are two different things, and I'm not sure I'm ready for what having her would mean.

KISS ME AGAIN

LOGAN

C hristmas Eve, and here I am, surrounded by more lights and holiday cheer than I thought one town could hold. Garland, twinkling lights, and those infernal Christmas tunes blaring from every corner. The kids are laughing, tugging at my red suit, asking for gifts they think Santa's going to slide under their tree tonight. And somehow, it's her fault that I'm even here.

Clara's buzzing around, that laugh of hers drifting through the air, contagious as anything. She's been at this festival for hours, cheering up kids, making parents laugh and somehow rallying half the town to turn this whole place into some kind of holiday wonderland. And I can't keep my eyes off her. She's standing over there in a deep green dress and matching hat, her cheeks pink from the cold and the constant movement. She's so...alive. And so damn hot.

It's hard to admit, but watching her like this, she almost makes me want to believe again. Almost.

The night starts to wind down, families head home, and the crowd thins. I'm not usually one for small talk, but I end up chatting with a few old faces from around town, and before I know it, it's just me and Clara packing up the last of the decorations. She turns and catches my eye. "Not so grumpy now, are you, Bad Santa?" She teases, that sparkle in her eye making her look like she just won a prize.

I roll my eyes, grumbling, but I can't help the smirk that pulls at my mouth. "Only because it's over. You finally worn out yet?"

She laughs, soft and easy, and something about that laugh makes me forget every single reason I've had for staying distant. The walls I've built for years suddenly don't seem so solid.

"Logan, you're practically a holiday miracle yourself. Who would've thought the town's Grinch would be out here, dressed as Santa, for Christmas Eve?" She steps closer, her eyes steady on mine. "You look...different tonight."

She's so close now I can see every speck of color in her eyes, feel the warmth radiating off her even in the cold. I'm lost in her scent, something sweet and warm, like vanilla. Her cheeks are flushed, her lips curved in a soft smile that makes my pulse jump.

"I don't hate it," I admit, my voice rough. "I mean, I hate the lights, the crowds, and the noise, but...being here with you?"

Her eyes flicker to my lips, and damn, it's like she's daring me. That pull I've felt since the start, that aggravating, infuriating attraction—it's ripping through me, stronger than ever. And then, without even thinking, I close the last bit of distance between us.

"Clara," I murmur, not even sure what I'm going to say. But then I don't have to because she steps closer, her breath catching as I reach out, my hand slipping around her waist. She tilts her face up, those big eyes locked on mine, and that look—sweet, like she's been waiting for this just as much as I have—it's all the invitation I need. I pull her flush against me, feeling the softness of her curves, and that's it. I'm done for.

I lower my mouth to hers, and the second our lips meet,

it's like something snaps. Her hands grip the front of my jacket, pulling me even closer, and my arms wrap around her, holding her tight, like if I let go, she might slip away.

The kiss is slow, deep, with every pent-up feeling I've shoved down finally finding a way out. She tastes like peppermint, sweet and intoxicating, and I can't get enough. My hand slides up her back, pressing her closer, letting her feel just how much I want her. Her fingers tangle in my hair, pulling me down as she leans up on her toes, meeting me kiss for kiss, spark for spark.

She pulls back just enough to breathe, her gaze hazy, lips swollen. "Logan," she whispers, her voice soft, but her eyes—those eyes—are anything but. They're daring me, challenging me to keep going. And hell, I'm not about to back down now.

"Been wanting to do that since the second I laid eyes on you," I admit, my voice rough and low. Our lips meet again, fiercer this time, the urgency between us sparking like live wire. Her hands slide up my arms, then around my neck, and all I can think is that I need more of her. Need her closer, need her warmth, her softness, everything she's offering me in this moment. She's my perfect contradiction—sugar and fire, softness and strength.

Finally, I pull back, just enough to look at her, my hand still tangled in her hair, thumb brushing along her jaw. "You have no idea what you're doing to me, Clara," I rasp, my heart pounding harder than it has in years.

She laughs, and it's the sweetest damn sound. "Just kiss me again, Logan."

THAT WAY...

LOGAN

The moment the door closes behind us, I can't take it anymore. I catch her in my arms, my lips crashing hungrily against hers. Clara moans into the kiss, her body molding against mine.

"Bedroom," she manages to gasp between kisses, her fingers feverishly tugging at my shirt buttons "That way..." she points.

I waste no time, sweeping her up into my arms and carrying her down the hallway. The bedroom is a haven of soft light and inviting scents, the perfect setting for what's to come. I lay her down on the bed, my eyes ravenous as they devour her flushed skin and heaving chest.

"You're so fucking beautiful," I growl, my fingers shaking as I undo the zip in her dress. She arches her back, allowing me better access. I slide the fabric off her body, revealing her creamy, porcelain skin, her curves driving me wild.

"Logan," she whispers, her voice a siren's call as I trail kisses down her collarbone. I need to taste every inch of her. My lips move lower, my tongue flicking against her hardened nipples.

"Oh, Logan, yes," she cries out, her nails digging into the sheets.

I continue, my hands exploring her body, memorizing every curve, every dip, and every arch. My hand slides between her thighs, and she's already wet with anticipation. I tease her folds, circling her clit with my fingertips, reveling in her whimpers and moans.

"I need you, Logan," she begs, her hips bucking against my hand.

I stand and shed my clothes, revealing my throbbing length. The look in her eyes consumes every ounce of control I thought I had left.

"Look at me, Clara," I command, my voice gruff with need. "Look into my eyes while I make you mine."

Clara's eyes lock onto mine as I position myself at her entrance. Slowly, achingly so, I pushed inside her hot, wet heat. Her body clamps down on mine, her nails digging into my back.

"Relax baby … let me in."

"Ohh, hmm…Lo..gan.."

I push further, my cock throbbing. The feeling of being inside her is unlike anything I'd ever experienced—as if every fiber of my being had been waiting for this very moment. "God, Clara," I groaned, fighting for control. "You feel... incredible."

Her response is a whimpered moan as she arches her hips upwards, urging me to go deeper. I oblige, my thrusts growing more insistent, more urgent with each passing second. The bedframe creaks in time with our frantic movements, the room filling with our mingled gasps and pants.

Her fingers tangled in my hair as she pulls me down for a kiss, her tongue teasing mine, our bodies speaking a language all their own—one that only we can understand.

"Logan," she moans against my lips. "Oh, Logan... I'm... I'm... Logan!" she cries out as her climax hits her like a freight train, her nails raking down my back as her contractions clenched around me like a vice grip.

Her orgasm sends me over the edge right behind her. I bury my face in the crook of her neck as wave after wave of ecstasy course through me, my entire world narrowing down to this single moment with her.

I collapse on top of her. "That was..." Words fail me, so I settle for brushing a damp strand of hair from her forehead instead.

She rewards me with a sated smile, her eyes glowing "I know," she breathes. "Merry Christmas."

GINGERBREAD AND COOKIES
CLARA

I pipe a perfect red Santa hat onto the last gingerbread man, admiring my handiwork. The warm, spicy scent of cinnamon and ginger fills the kitchen as I set down the piping bag and step back to survey the cookie army lined up on the counter. Each one wears a jaunty hat and sports a jolly smile – the epitome of Christmas cheer.

A floorboard creaks behind me. I turn around and wipe my flour-dusted hands on my apron. There's Logan standing in the doorway. My breath catches at the sight of him. Memories of last night flood back."Merry Christmas," he says. He's holding a small box wrapped with a simple red bow. "Didn't get the chance to give you this last night."

My cheeks flush as I recall exactly why he didn't have a chance. "I, um..." I stammer. Logan's eyes crinkle with amusement at my awkwardness. I clear my throat and try again. "Merry Christmas to you, too."

A gift? What could it be? When did he get it? What does it mean?

I smile, reaching for his hand and pulling him inside. "Merry Christmas, Logan." His fingers are warm against mine, and I have to resist the urge to intertwine them fully.

Instead, I release his hand and turn towards the counter, my heart racing.

"Here," I say, picking up one of the freshly decorated cookies. "Try this." I hold it out to him, watching as he takes it, his rough fingers brushing against mine.

Logan bites into the cookie, and I find myself holding my breath, waiting for his reaction. "Pretty good," he says, nodding in that understated way of his.

"Just pretty good?" I tease, trying to keep my tone light. "I'll have you know these are my grandmother's secret recipe." I give him a playful shove, my hand connecting with his solid, naked chest.

"Okay, okay, best damn cookie I've ever had." He grins, setting down the box on the counter, and I can see something in his eyes I didn't see before. A softness, a warmth. And maybe...something deeper. Maybe, just maybe, it was more than just one night...

I tug at the ribbon and lift the lid to find a small, simple snow globe inside. A little replica of our town square, complete with the giant Christmas tree in the center.

"Logan, this is..." I trail off, unable to find the right words. Instead, I give the globe a gentle shake, watching as tiny flecks of glitter swirl around the scene. "It's beautiful," I whisper, looking up at him.

He reaches out, tucking a strand of hair behind my ear, his eyes steady on mine. "So's the woman who makes it all happen."

"And here I thought you didn't believe in Christmas miracles," I say, running a hand down his chest. I can feel his heart racing beneath my palm. My own pulse quickens in response.

Logan's eyes darken and he leans in close, his breath hot against my ear. "I don't," he murmurs, his voice low and husky, sending shivers down my spine. "But I believe in this."

He grips my waist and lifts me onto the kitchen counter. The cool marble contrasts sharply with the heat of his touch.

My breath catches in my throat as he steps between my legs, his hands sliding up my thighs.

I draw him closer with my arms around his neck. The scent of pine and cinnamon surrounds us—a heady mix of Logan and Christmas. My heart pounces so loudly that I'm sure he must hear it.

"Logan," I whisper, my voice trembling. This response is a deep, rumbling growl vibrating through my entire body. He slides inside me and I melt into him, my fingers tangling in his hair as I pull him even closer. His kiss deepens, and I can taste the sweetness of the gingerbread cookie on his tongue. He breaks the kiss, his lips tracing a path along my jaw and down my neck, his hands roaming my body. I gasp as he finds a particularly sensitive spot. He pounds into me, slowly and steady, savouring each thrust. Oh God!

As we catch our breath afterward, still tangled together, I can't help but laugh softly.

"What's so funny?" Logan asks, nuzzling my neck.

I gesture at the mess of flour and icing surrounding us. "I think we've ruined Christmas cookies forever."

He grins, "I'd say we've made them even sweeter." And then lets out a slow breath as if he's building up the courage to say something big. "Clara, you make me believe in...things I thought I'd lost a long time ago. Family, happiness, maybe even...home."

"Me too," I admit breathlessly. "I never thought..."

He pulls back slightly, his eyes searching mine. "Never thought what?"

I cup his face in my hands, overwhelmed by the motion I see reflected there. "That you'd feel the same way."

A smile tugs at his lips. "How could I not? Miss Christmas? Bad Santa?" His voice is tender and filled with a warmth that makes my heart swell. "I'm not letting you go, ever. You're mine now."

EPILOGUE
LOGAN

S now dusts the streets of Berryville, covering the rooftops and blanketing the town square in soft white. It's almost a perfect mirror of last year's Christmas festival, but this time, everything is different.

Clara's hand is wrapped up in mine, her gloved fingers warm against my palm, and as we walk past the booths and lights, she smiles up at me, eyes twinkling like every Christmas light in town was captured just for her. It's still strange how one person managed to get me tangled up in this holiday magic, but she's been getting me tangled since the moment she told me I was playing Santa.

I glance around, the familiar bustle and cheer of the crowd settling in my chest in a way that feels oddly...good. Comfortable, even. Never thought I'd feel it again after everything that happened, but Clara has a way of pulling you in and not letting go.

"So," I say, nudging her lightly with my shoulder. "Didn't get enough of roping me into last year's Santa duties? Because I'm about two seconds from starting a petition to get someone else in that red suit."

"Oh, please," she laughs, rolling her eyes. "You're the best

Bad Santa this town has ever had," she says with a mischievous glint, tapping my chest. "Grumpy and gruff. Plus, you look pretty cute in a Santa suit."

I chuckle, shaking my head. "Well, you better enjoy it while you can. After we're married, the only person I'm playing Santa for is you."

We make our way over to the pavilion, where she finally lets go of my hand to adjust a stray strand of garland on the railing. I watch her, still all warmth and cheer even after a full day of organizing this town circus. She's... *my* everything.

Clara glances back at me, eyes softening as I step up to her. "What?" she asks, eyebrow raised in that teasing way that always does a number on me.

It's just us under the string lights. I tilt her chin up, catching her gaze before I press my lips to hers, slow and easy. I pull back, and she's looking up at me like she did the first time I kissed her under those same lights. "I can't believe I actually got you to love Christmas," she says softly like it's a secret just between us.

"Correction," I murmur, brushing my thumb along her cheek. "You got me to love you."

With her, every day feels like Christmas.

GET YOUR FREE EBOOK

Sign up the Laura (L.A.) Mariani mailing list for a FREE steamy romance.

You'll be the first to hear about new releases, exclusive offers, bonus content and all Laura's news. You can even email her back. She loves chatting with her readers!

To claim your free ebook visit:
    https://laura-mariani-author.ck.page/freeshortstory

AUTHOR'S NOTE

Thank you so much for reading **Angels & Demons**.

I hope you enjoyed the stories. A review would be much appreciated as it helps other readers discover the story. Or a few stars perhaps - the more the better ;-) !

Thanks.

Laura xx

ABOUT THE AUTHOR

Laura Alexandra (L.A.) Mariani is a best selling author of Short & Steamy Romance | Where Alpha Males Meet Fierce Heroines for Sweet Endings, your go-to author for captivating romance tales that will sweep you off your feet and keep you on the edge of your seat!

When Laura is not weaving stories of love, desire and suspense, you'll find her exploring the vibrant streets of London, drawing inspiration from its hidden corners and bustling markets, or strolling through the charming streets of Paris, savoring street food in Rome, or relaxing on a sun-kissed beach in Bali, her journeys fuelling her creativity and infuse her stories with wanderlust.

You can also follow her on

      𝕏 x.com/PeopleAlchemist
      ⊙ instagram.com/lauramariani_author

Printed in Great Britain
by Amazon